# Travis couldn't shake the prickly feeling of being watched.

If he and Casey were still together, he'd have suggested a quick run to the coast, a dinner of sandwiches and soda while they dug their toes in the sand. It was half on his tongue to ask, but probably wasn't a smart idea.

"You look like you're plotting something." Casey had stopped at the edge of the brick sidewalk and was eyeballing him like she really could read his thoughts.

That would be scary.

He looked both ways, waiting for a break in traffic. "Me? Plotting? Not at all."

An older Nissan 280ZX stopped half a block away and flashed its lights.

Travis and Casey both threw a wave of thanks and stepped into the street, aiming for Travis's truck on the other side.

A sudden squeal tore the air.

Adrenaline crashed through him in a lightning jolt of pain as the Nissan roared straight for them.

**Jodie Bailey** writes novels about freedom and the heroes who fight for it. Her novel *Crossfire* won a 2015 RT Reviewers' Choice Best Book Award. She is convinced a camping trip to the beach with her family, a good cup of coffee and a great book can cure all ills. Jodie lives in North Carolina with her husband, her daughter and two dogs.

## Books by Jodie Bailey

### Love Inspired Suspense

*Freefall*
*Crossfire*
*Smokescreen*
*Compromised Identity*
*Breach of Trust*
*Dead Run*
*Calculated Vendetta*

# CALCULATED VENDETTA

## JODIE BAILEY

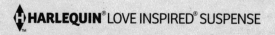

HARLEQUIN® LOVE INSPIRED® SUSPENSE

Recycling programs
for this product may
not exist in your area.

LOVE INSPIRED BOOKS

ISBN-13: 978-0-373-45706-9

Calculated Vendetta

www.Harlequin.com

**Printed in U.S.A.**

There is no fear in love; but perfect love casteth out fear:
because fear hath torment.
He that feareth is not made perfect in love.
*−1 John* 4:18

To Mom, who taught me to see God in all things,
big and small. Because of you, I see Him everywhere I go.

# ONE

The conversations of the late dinner crowd in the Mexican restaurant hummed around Staff Sergeant Casey Jordan as she loaded one more chip with salsa and promised herself this one—like the eight before it—would be the real "last one." Probably not, but still… Didn't she deserve to indulge a little after her dinner companion had excused himself to take his fourth phone call in twenty minutes? Finally, she'd given up and told John Winslow they could reschedule, and he'd taken off for the door after a quick *thanks* and a wave.

Sure, it wasn't technically a date, rather an interview for the story she was working on for the Fort Bragg Public Affairs Office, but the diners around them had no idea of that. To them, she'd been royally disrespected.

Reaching for the chip basket, Casey chose a perfect triangle. One more, then she'd throw in the napkin and go home to the cliché of pajamas, ice cream and the hardest sudoku puzzle she could lay her hands on. After her last relationship had spectacularly flamed out, she deserved all the comfort food she could get.

"Casey?" The sound of her name rose above the other noises in the small restaurant. For a second, her hopes rose, but they crashed to the floor just as quickly. The voice was definitely not John's.

It was her own thoughts come to life in flesh and blood.

She did her best to ignore the call as her stomach tightened around the chips she'd downed. Not now. This was the last thing she needed on a night when it looked as though a date had abandoned her. Way to drive the knife in, making *him* appear.

Grabbing the backpack that held her laptop, Casey slung it over her shoulder, pretending she hadn't heard Travis Heath hailing her. It had been three months, and he hadn't called her once. Let him enjoy the burn of being ignored. She'd rather go home and dig into a pint of Mackinac Island Fudge than make small talk with the guy who'd gotten her hopes up before he ground them into mush under the heel of his combat boot.

Then again, knowing Travis, ignoring him would only make him more persistent. Better to face the past than have it chase her out of the restaurant and become the dinner show for an audience chowing on tacos and chips.

When she stopped near the counter and turned, Travis ran right into her. He grabbed her upper arms to steady both of them, forcing Casey to look at him fully for the first time.

Yep. He was everything she remembered. Tall. Lean but muscular. Blue-eyed under slightly longer-than-regulation dark blond hair. If she glanced around the restaurant now, half the women there would be staring at him. Casey inhaled and tried not to notice he still smelled like outdoors and ocean, even though the coast was nearly two hours away.

Scent recall was definitely a thing, because the slightest whiff of him brought an assault of memories that threatened to drag her right back to him. For a second, she'd glimpsed the old him, the him she'd loved.

But he'd hurt her, and being nice to him wasn't on the agenda.

She didn't even bother to fake a civil smile. "Travis."

"Casey." He scanned her face slowly, like he was soaking her in, but then he blinked and glanced over her shoulder at the door. "The guy you were having dinner with. Was he John Winslow?"

She edged closer to the counter to pay. Hopefully her cheeks hadn't turned as red as they felt. Casey focused on his question, trying to ignore the way he folded the past into the present. What did it matter to him whom she had dinner with? He didn't have the right to ask.

"It was." She made a show of glancing at her watch and then over her shoulder at the door, as though she had somewhere so much better to be. "And I have to go." Sidestepping him, she pulled her arms from his warm grasp, trying not to make the action as slow and reluctant as she felt. The tiny little traitor inside her wanted to stay right where she was. Good thing her intellect was stronger than her heart. "See you around."

Travis opened his mouth and closed it again, watching her like he couldn't quite figure out if she was serious about walking away. "How did you meet John?"

He couldn't really believe he had the right to ask such a question. "Really not any of your business, is it?" Casey turned away and forced a smile at the cashier. There was nothing to talk about, especially if it was the way he'd spotted her across the room and suddenly remembered she existed. Or he'd decided to be jealous because somebody else wanted to be with her.

Except John didn't have any more interest in hanging around than Travis had. She huffed out her frustration and headed for the exit without looking back.

Travis didn't follow, but she knew he watched her as she pushed through the front door. Pent-up anger roiled inside her. If he was the kind of man who could be trusted, he wouldn't have taken off on her with some lame excuse about the army not being conducive to a family. She was as much of a soldier as he was, and that was the flimsiest reason in the world for a breakup.

Outside, she inhaled deeply and immediately wished she hadn't. The humidity of the early September evening made taking a breath feel more like drowning. It was after eight o'clock, but the heat of the day held on even in the twilight. It didn't matter she'd been raised here, nobody ever really got used to the way summer dragged into autumn. The North Carolina Sandhills brought with them a special kind of humidity-fueled torture.

Grabbing her phone, she started to fire off a text to John to cancel their interview for the next day, but she paused. He'd been a great source on her last article, and his input would be valuable for her research on the Joint Task Force mission he'd been a part of five years ago. Casey tapped her thumb against her phone. This was why business and personal didn't mix.

Maybe she should let it go. This was one working dinner with a man she hardly knew. Nothing serious.

Casey glanced over her shoulder. Nothing like the place she'd been with Travis when he walked out her door for the last time.

Forget him. Forget this day. She was done. Casey shoved her phone into her hip pocket and pulled her keys from her purse. Time to go home to air-conditioning and ice cream.

"Casey, wait."

Against her will, her feet dragged to a stop on the sidewalk. Yep. Travis was still tenacious.

And she still couldn't resist him.

Travis stopped beside her and glanced around the parking lot. "At least let me walk you to your car. If John can't be gentleman enough to—"

"Are you for real?" Casey whipped around and turned the full force of her pent-up fury on him. "Were you watching the whole time? You think you get to spy on me because…because why, exactly? Walk away, Travis. Seems like that's the one thing you're really good at."

He didn't back off like she'd expected but held his ground, his expression neutral. "Just walking you to your car, Case. Let a guy be nice, okay?"

Travis was a lot of things, including a big kid in a man's body, but one thing was certain—his mama had taught him how to be a gentleman. He'd walk any lone female to her car. It had nothing to do with her. She could stand on the sidewalk and fight him, or she could let him take the walk to the end of the row with her, thank him, then go on her not-so-merry way.

It was easier to give in. Without another word, she turned on her heel, made sure no cars were coming, then stepped off the sidewalk.

Travis kept pace beside her, not saying a word.

As much as she didn't want to talk to him, Casey couldn't hack the silence. Between the two of them, it was unnatural. She tightened her grip on the strap of her backpack, running her thumb along the stitching. "Did you ever get any word on orders?" He should have moved on from Bragg months ago, but an investigation at his unit had held all his soldiers in place. Word around post was the fence was down now that the investigation was closed, and guys were being shuffled to other assignments.

He lagged behind then caught up, as though the question had slowed his pace. "I—" He cleared his throat. "I'm going to selection for a Special Missions Unit in a little over a week."

"I never knew you wanted to go that route." There were a lot of things he'd kept from her, including his apparent fear of commitment.

"You still with the Public Affairs Office?" He didn't answer her question, and she didn't push it.

"I am." They'd reached her Jeep and Casey stopped, staring at the door handle as she slipped the backpack from her shoulders. Turning to look at him would be dangerous. Her pride was already bruised by John. She didn't need the reminder of what could have been if she let herself look at Travis Heath long enough to remember he wasn't the root of all evil. "I'll probably be there until—"

There was movement at the front of her Jeep, and someone melted out of the shadows. Surely John wasn't waiting, thinking he could shoehorn his way into her evening once again.

She turned her back fully to Travis, facing the newcomer.

It wasn't John. A man appeared at the front of her SUV, a hood over his head casting his face into shadow, and a pistol pointed straight at her chest.

Travis's muscles tightened, the heat of confrontation rushing through him. It took all he had not to shove Casey to safety and rush the guy. Instead, he edged between her and the gunman and balled his fists, forcing his attention from the pistol to the man, trying to size his advantage and figure out the best way to get Casey safely out of this.

In spite of the heat, their attacker wore a dark hoodie pulled forward to distort his features in shadow. Still, something about him was vaguely familiar, a flicker of memory Travis couldn't grasp.

Now wasn't the time to try.

The gun wavered from Travis to Casey, almost as though the man holding it wasn't quite sure what to do next.

Travis eased one foot forward, getting himself in position to take out the foe, but the pistol stabilized, aimed squarely at him.

*Whoa.* Travis froze, reading confusion in the gunman's expression. This guy was no pro, but he wasn't a novice either. Rather than aiming at the head, he had the pistol pointed squarely at center mass, the mark of someone who had at least a little training. Something told Travis the guy could probably get off a fairly accurate shot, but that wasn't a theory he wanted to test.

He'd trained for moments like this, but having Casey thrown into the mix complicated everything. Right now, Travis was physically trapped with the Jeep on one side and a car on the other, but he'd always been better with his words anyway. "Dude, you don't have to do anything crazy."

The statement hardened the man's resolve, and his stance stiffened. "I want her backpack...and your wallet."

"Take it easy." He'd hand over everything in his possession as long as the guy didn't pull the trigger on Casey. The barrel of a weapon aimed straight at them made Travis willing to do whatever it took to protect her.

But he had an idea. "Casey, hand me your backpack." He lowered his right arm slowly, like he was reaching behind him for the bag.

The gunman steadied his aim.

Behind Travis, Casey hesitated, giving him a second to pray she wouldn't choose this moment to argue, then she slipped the strap into his hand.

Perfect.

Travis wrapped his fingers around the canvas strap and eased forward, bracing himself for whatever came next. If this was the last breath he took, at least he could say he'd given it all he had. He threw his arm out, the backpack catching their assailant in the arm.

The gun clattered off the trunk of the car beside them and Travis rushed forward, but the narrow space between the Jeep and the car slowed his momentum.

The other man snatched Casey's backpack, skirted the front of the Jeep and ran for a dark sedan idling two spaces away, leaving tire rubber in the parking lot as Travis skidded to a halt, trying in vain to read the license plate before distance made it impossible.

No good. The car was moving too fast and the lights weren't bright enough.

Travis slammed a fist into the side of his leg, then turned and ran to Casey, his heart racing from adrenaline and exertion. If anything had happened to her...

She sat on the running board of her Jeep, face buried in her hands.

Travis knelt in front of her and rested his hands on her knees. Even though the weapon hadn't been fired, relief still washed over him at the sight of her. "You okay?"

Her whole body moved with the effort of breathing. "Give me a minute."

Easing away, Travis stood and pulled his phone from his pocket to call the police. He let his free hand rest on the back of Casey's head, running his fingers through the loose blond strands that fell forward to cover her cheeks, the softness cascading across hands that shook from the adrenaline of the chase. How to handle this? He couldn't put an arm around her to hug her. She'd probably deck him. But he also couldn't let her suffer alone.

When he ended the call, Casey slipped her hair from his fingers and looked at him, her gray eyes cloaked in an emotion he couldn't read. "I'm not your dog. You can stop petting me."

In spite of the situation, Travis bit down on a grin. That was exactly what he'd been doing. Hey, it had worked for Harley the shelter mutt back in the day, when his family had ridden out hurricanes on the Florida Panhandle. And it had worked for Gus, the dog he'd had to give up when he deployed the last time. He ignored the ache the Australian shepherd's memory brought. He always lost the things he loved. Life somehow seemed to work that way. "Are you sure you're not hurt? What was in your backpack?"

"My laptop." She gave him a weak smile. "He's in for a surprise. The battery's dead and the charger's at my apartment."

Casey was as sarcastic as she'd ever been, a quality she tended to amp to a thousand under stress. He'd encountered the trait more than once when her best friend was under the gun in February. "Bad day for him, huh?"

"For sure." She dipped her chin and stared at the pavement between her feet, growing serious. "You know, if you hadn't walked me out…"

Travis glanced toward the sky, grateful for the nudge that had sent him after her. If something had happened to her while he licked his wounds inside, he'd never have been able to forgive himself. He eased to the running board beside her, wary of touching her after her reaction. Running a hand down his face, he winced at the realization of what she'd lost. She kept her life on her phone and her laptop. Losing the machine would be a blow. "Were you working on anything?"

"An article on…" She froze, then waved her hand as though the question were a buzzing mosquito. "No big deal. Everything's saved in the cloud, so it's all retrievable. The machine's password protected, so I doubt he can do much with it anyway." Her hand fluttered up and fell. "It's the hassle of having to deal with insurance and then finding the time to buy a new one. And knowing somebody held a gun on us and now has my whole digital life in their hands…" A shudder shook her, the biggest since she'd bucked up and tried to act like this whole incident was no big deal.

Travis slipped an arm around her as two police cars roared into the parking lot, sirens blaring. He couldn't let her sit here and fight this internal battle by herself. And when she leaned into him he knew...

He was in this for as long as she needed him.

# TWO

"You didn't need to come over. Really." Casey tried to block the doorway to keep her best friend from entering the apartment. There was a reason she hadn't called Kristin James and told her what had happened at the restaurant. Casey had known it would go down exactly like this, with her stubborn friend practically bursting through the door.

Casey didn't want a babysitter. She wanted a quiet place to curl into a ball and fall apart in peace. The shudders that had fluttered through her like wild birds for the past couple of hours were trying their best to work their way out to every limb. When she let go, the force would likely be epic, and the last thing an explosion of such a magnitude needed was a witness.

Of course, Kristin was having none of that. She slipped past Casey into the small hardwood entryway, dropping her backpack into the doorway of the guest room as she passed. "Seems to me I remember the same argument coming out of my own mouth a few months ago." She crossed her arms. "Did you leave me alone when someone came at me and broke into my house? No. I'm pretty sure I remember you bunking in my guest room and, oh, calling the police even though I asked you not to."

Casey crossed her own arms and mimicked her friend's posture. "Your brother pasted a target on your back. This is different. Tonight was a random mugging."

"With a gun." Kristin stepped into her personal space and leaned even closer. "Don't pretend everything's all sunshine and roses."

"Like you did?" Jerking away, Casey stalked for the den. Kristin had no room to talk. When the smuggler her brother had double-crossed came calling, Kristin hadn't wanted help either, even after she was attacked in her own home. "If I want to be alone right now, let's say I learned from the best."

"Ooh. Ouch." Kristin twisted the dead bolt then followed Casey, her relentless streak going full bore. "See? This is how I know you're not fine. You're not me. You don't go around biting heads off."

She was right, for the most part. "Maybe I'm not like you in some ways. But in others..." Casey dropped onto the couch and stared at the ceiling.

"You need to be alone to cry." Settling onto the opposite end of the creamy beige sofa, Kristin smiled with a gentleness out of character for her. Rarely did her blue eyes soften with sympathy. "I get it."

"Yet you're still not leaving."

"Nope."

"How did you find out anyway?"

Kristin's eyebrow arched. "Two guesses."

"Travis called Lucas." Casey sighed. She should have known without asking. Kristin's fiancé, Lucas Murphy, was platoon sergeant in the same company as

Travis. They'd been close friends for years. It shouldn't surprise her Travis had contacted his best friend, who'd turned right around and contacted hers. After all, they'd met through the other couple, and although Casey had managed to avoid Travis for months, her days of avoiding him had likely run out.

"I never understood why the two of you didn't work out."

"You'd have to ask him." While Casey appreciated Kristin trying to change the subject, she'd a thousand times rather talk about the mugging than her non-existent relationship with Travis Heath. He'd been fun, had made her laugh, had been a perfect gentleman. Then one day, he was simply gone. The thought of his departure still burned bitter. "So how's the wedding planning coming along?"

Kristin's lips tightened into a thin line. Clearly, she didn't want to change the subject.

Getting engaged had softened her hard edges so much that she now thought the rest of the world should pair up, too. Even though it had been months since Travis quit their relationship, Kristin still held out hope her best friend and Lucas's best friend would somehow form their own happy little family. She sighed. "Wedding planning is good. We're going for simple. Small. You don't come around enough anymore."

So they were back to that. Well, she didn't like being the third wheel. "Busy. And you ought not to be here. You should be out with Lucas, cuddling in a coffee shop or running a marathon or something."

"I don't cuddle in public, and we ran this morning." Kristin laughed, the sound a bright light in the apartment that suddenly seemed dim. "Besides, it's past midnight. Lucas better be at his house sound asleep."

"And you should be at your house sound asleep, too."

"I've got better things to do." Reaching across the small gap between them, Kristin aimed a finger at Casey. "Like it or not, it's a good thing Travis was with you. If the guy had a gun, he was serious."

A shudder quivered Casey's insides as she pictured the tense posture of the man who'd aimed that pistol. How much different would her night be right now if Travis hadn't insisted on being a gentleman? She could have lost more than her laptop.

"I knew it would hit you." Sliding closer, Kristin leaned her shoulder against Casey's. Kristin had never been a touchy-feely person, but she knew how to help carry a load, especially since she'd found Lucas and Jesus. The change had taken some getting used to, but her friend was definitely happier now than she had been in previous years.

"I can't stop the video." Casey's voice quavered, but she didn't care. Let Kristin hear it. She was safe here. "I fought Travis on walking me to my car. If he'd listened to me and backed off..."

"But he didn't. You're right here, safe in your own apartment."

Leave it to Kristin to hit her with a truth she couldn't deny. Casey shoved aside the what-ifs. It was better to focus on the actuallys, which were a little bit easier to handle. "He took my laptop."

"You mean your right arm?" Thankfully, Kristin followed her down the rabbit trail away from nightmares. "You had a backup, I hope."

"I have my old machine to use until I can buy another, and everything is backed up on an external disk and in the cloud, but it's still a pain. It'll take a whole day to sort everything out and put it all together again."

"Well, before you do that, you ought to spend some time out on your great-grandfather's farm with your bow."

"Wouldn't that be nice?" It would feel good to pull back the string and let fly at a few targets. Really good. Load the fear and the stress into the tension of the string then release it forever.

It was a nice dream, but there was too much work to do. "Can't. I'm wrapping up an interview with John Winslow tomorrow, and I have one with another guy the day after tomorrow." No need to discuss John's behavior tonight. She hadn't even told Kristin there was a dinner. Confessing would bring too many questions Casey didn't know how to answer.

She'd met John a year earlier, when she was writing an article about substance abuse among army veterans. He'd introduced her to a few other sources, and one of them had suggested the article she was working on now. When she'd contacted him again about discussing a mission he'd been on a few years ago, he'd been interested in everything she had to say, asking questions and talking for hours when they met for their first interview two days ago. He'd been the one to ask her to meet him for dinner instead of at her office, so the water was a little muddy when it came to what to call tonight. Especially since he kept disappearing with his phone, more distracted every time he returned to the table until she'd cut him loose.

"At least you won't have to restart your story."

"Thankfully." Casey had already conducted interviews with two soldiers and had several more in-person and telephone interviews lined up... All except the one she'd rather not schedule at all. If she'd lost all her work, had lost her contacts or her calendar... She let her eyes drift shut, focusing on the averted technology disaster over the averted physical one. "The laptop's locked, so everything's safe, but still, the idea somebody has my stuff..."

"It's violating. I know. I felt the same way when someone broke into my car and stole my keys last year. Even after I changed the locks, it still felt like somebody was creeping around in the dark corners of my house."

"Well, they were."

"Yeah, but—"

On the coffee table, Casey's phone vibrated on the glass. Kristin reached for it and glanced at the screen, then turned it toward Casey. "Travis is calling you."

"Let it ring." Right now, she was too vulnerable, too willing to let her fear and overwrought emotions fool her into thinking he was the one who got away, that everything would be so much better if she had him beside her right now, holding her close while she leaned on his strong shoulder the way he'd let her at the crime scene.

Kristin dropped the phone onto the coffee table with a clatter. "If you don't answer, he's coming over here. You know how he is. He was worried enough when he called Lucas."

"Text him and tell him you're here and all is well."

"Casey..."

"Just do it. I can't talk to him right now."

Kristin fired off a text, clearly irritated, then shoved the device onto the table beside Casey's. "He's a good guy. No matter what's happened between you in the past, you owe him a thank-you for being there tonight."

Casey begged to differ about him being *a good guy*, but yeah, she did owe him a thank-you for being a hero if nothing else. But when it came to forgiving him? It would take a whole lot more than him playing superhero.

Travis dropped his cell phone to the desk and stared out the window at the small strip of trees standing guard behind his apartment building. He missed the beach, the deep darkness over water where the only light came from the moon and stars. Living in a land-locked town might allow him to be close to post, but it didn't give him a whole lot of opportunities to indulge his appreciation for nature.

He should have joined the navy, then he'd have had all the water he ever wanted. Whole oceans of it.

But he wouldn't have been in place to help Lucas when he stared down danger in February. And he wouldn't have been in place tonight to save Casey Jordan from a man who may have wanted money or something more. He still wasn't sure which. All he could see when he closed his eyes was the gun, pointed unwaveringly at both of them.

He'd seen the aftermath of violence before. Had watched a good soldier and a better friend take the hit right in front of him, an image that overlaid tonight's near-tragedy in rivers of blood. Sergeant Neil Aiken had been one of the best, and he'd died right in front of Travis, leaving a wife and two little ones behind to face the world without him.

And he'd still be here today if it hadn't been for Travis's foolish mistake.

Travis's arms still bore scars from the shrapnel, but he'd survived. Had he been at the head of his team like he should have been, he'd have been the one to plant a boot in the wrong place.

Pulse pounding, Travis jerked the cord on the blinds and shut out the world. In a couple of weeks, he'd pack his bags and go to selection, then on to training for the Special Missions Unit that would take him far away from here.

And far away from Casey Jordan. For a few months with her, he'd let himself believe he could hold her close without getting attached. Then one day, the danger of such a belief hit him from the left. He'd been at her apartment, sitting on the couch with her snuggled beside him, watching some silly rom-com, his fingers toying with the ends of her hair... In the perfect peace of the moment, he'd known a depth of emotion he'd never felt before. It quaked something inside him, and when he'd kissed her goodbye he'd felt a kind of desperate, indefinable something that made him want to cling to her forever.

That night, his nightmares had amped their intensity, walking him again and again through the horrible day he'd been injured and Neil Aiken had died. He'd paced the floor in a desperate blend of guilt and fear that had made him want to claw at his own skin. He couldn't love a woman like Casey. Couldn't let her take over his life. He had too much to pay for sending one of his men ahead of him to die.

The next morning he'd texted Casey to tell her they were finished, full of lame excuses, aware such disrespect was the coward's way out but knowing he could never go through with it if he heard her voice.

Now she'd reappeared in time to bring a deluge of memories with her.

In time to remind him of everything he'd lost when he walked away from her. If anything, she was more beautiful than he remembered. Casey's gray eyes still had the ability to stop him where he stood, those same eyes that had made other men look twice when they saw her, something she never seemed to notice. Her blond hair had grown longer, though it still didn't quite touch her shoulders. Shoulders that came to his chest, a fit he'd never known before or since.

But the fit had been all wrong.

Adrenaline and memories wouldn't let him sleep anytime soon—if at all—so Travis poured a tall glass of soda and only wished for a second he had something stronger to mix in. He'd been down that road after Neil Aiken died, hard and heavy. Drinking hadn't solved anything, hadn't brought anybody back from the dead. It had made the memories worse and his thoughts exponentially more morbid.

So instead of wallowing in the past, he'd tried to call Casey. After seeing death charge her this evening, all he wanted was to hear her voice one more time, to reassure himself he'd succeeded in saving her. If he knew she was okay, he could put all of this to rest again and go on with his life without her.

But she wasn't answering her phone, having Kristin text him instead of doing it herself. It shouldn't cut, but it did.

She was probably upset with him for going behind her back to call Kristin, but that was fine. It wasn't like things between them could get worse. She hadn't spoken to him in months anyway. Not that she should. He'd been the one to walk away. He'd had to, and he couldn't give her an explanation without making everything harder than it already was.

Travis took a long draw from his Pepsi and eyed the TV. Noise. Distraction. Anything would be better than the racket inside his own head.

His phone screamed from the desk, and he set the drink beside it, answering the call right before it went to voice mail. Casey. Desperate to know she was really still there, he didn't even bother with a hello. "You doing okay?"

The question stopped whatever she'd planned to say. She stuttered, then fell silent before she spoke. "Yeah, I am now. I wanted to thank you for stepping in." Her voice was uncharacteristically subdued. "You could have been shot."

"So could you." The thought brought those same fears he'd felt the night he'd left her. His leg muscles tensed, and he fought to relax. She really was safe. Things had worked out…this time. "Just the simple actions of your everyday superhero, ma'am."

She chuckled low. "I see you haven't changed a bit."

"I'm proud of that, if it's a good thing. I promise to change immediately if it's not."

"You're making my point for me."

He'd keep making it, too, if she'd keep laughing, would keep chasing away the dark. In the past, she'd brought out the better man who lived inside him.

Seemed like she still had the same ability. "Sorry I couldn't save your laptop."

"No worries. I get to spend tomorrow afternoon resetting my old one after I interview a guy for the article I'm working on."

"You're sure your laptop has a password?"

"Of course. It's mine. I logged into it every day."

"Good." He winced. This was all the opposite of how it used to be. When he'd met Casey, they'd clicked immediately, from the moment she'd walked through Lucas's front door and joined him on a pizza run. This? This was nowhere near the easy way they'd once fallen into. The discordance was his fault, and it stung in ways that made his palms sweat. "What's your article about?"

"Nothing very interesting." The way her voice dropped said differently.

"I doubt it. Tell me." Not that he needed to know, but he wasn't ready to stop talking and face his empty apartment again. He dropped into his desk chair and propped his feet on the windowsill.

She sighed in what sounded like defeat. "A Joint Task Force North mission on the Mexican border five years ago."

Travis gripped the phone tighter. The shot was too close to the target for comfort. If she was talking with John Winslow, one of his former soldiers, it meant this was all about his mission. His team. "The one we ran with Border Patrol, when we rounded up enough henchmen to put an upstart cartel out of business?" He struggled to keep his voice level. She knew he'd been a team leader on the mission and she hadn't even called to ask him for an interview.

No. Instead she'd called John Winslow. Awesome.

But that also meant she was with John tonight not because they were together, but because of her job. Her admission brought a warmth to his chilled bones. Only because she was safe from a self-proclaimed skirt chaser. Really, that was the only reason. Winslow was arrogant. Cocky. He collected women and tossed them aside as soon as he got tired of them, and it was usually faster than most people could imagine.

Travis winced. Kind of like he'd done a long, long time ago. "So tonight was an interview?"

"Tonight was dinner."

"Oh." His mood deflated. A date. She'd had a date. With Winslow.

Not only had she been out with a guy unworthy of her, it was one of his former soldiers to boot. The more he thought about it, the faster his fingers drummed the desk. "You could have interviewed me. I led the team."

"I know."

But she hadn't called him. No explanation. No reason. Just *I know.* Maybe he deserved it.

Maybe it still burned anyway.

"I'm meeting him tomorrow afternoon at his house to go over—"

"I'll go with you." He'd take off work if he had to. No way was she going to meet Winslow at his house alone. The guy was smooth, and Casey was trusting. He'd have her head spun around so fast…

"Absolutely not." Her words were as forceful as Travis had ever heard them.

Like a typical soldier, she'd never liked being bossed around in her personal life. He had to play this differently. "I haven't seen Winslow in a couple of years, not since right before I last deployed. Didn't even get a chance to speak to him tonight before he left. Would be a pretty interesting reunion." To say the least.

Casey was quiet again, but this time, it was the kind of quiet that said she was considering his proposal.

"Think about it. You could interview me, too, and if John and I get talking, it might jog even more memories. You and I wouldn't have to be alone. There would be somebody else there. I was the team leader. I can give you insight."

He knew playing the reunion card would tug at her, and the prospect of a more fruitful interview would seal the deal. It tweaked his conscience a little, pretending he and John were better buddies than they had been, but she'd be a whole lot safer with backup beside her.

"You know what? Fine. I'm meeting him at one. I'll text you the address and meet you there."

"Nah, I'll come by your place half an hour before. I'll talk to you later." He cut the call before she could protest, knowing her mother's manners were instilled in her deeply enough to keep her from leaving before he got there.

Travis dropped the phone on his desk and spun it in a quick circle. Keeping his distance would be hard, but he couldn't leave her alone now. He had to protect Casey when she went to interview John, keeping her safe from another guy who would break her heart.

# THREE

Casey tapped the download button and settled in to watch the app she used for notes load onto her new laptop. The whole morning had been consumed with stopping at the Post Exchange on her way in to buy a new computer and backpack, then downloading and resetting everything to her liking. Around her, the office was fairly silent, typical of a Friday. Most of the staff were busy at their desks or out working on various assignments. Casey and a couple of others sat in their cubicles, typing stories or conducting phone interviews.

She dragged her hands down her cheeks and rubbed eyes burning from lack of sleep, then reached for the mug on the warmer on her desk. The amount of caffeine she'd consumed today probably bordered on the danger zone, but it sure wasn't helping to keep her awake. All it had done was serve to make her already-bouncing nerves more jumpy.

She'd hardly slept, certain every stray sound in the apartment was the man with his gun coming to finish the job. There was zero evidence the attack was personal, but somewhere in the darkest part of the night, her brain had grown convinced a shadow had followed her home and was waiting for her to fall asleep before he crept into her private space to finish the job.

If it hadn't been for Kristin bunking in the spare room, Casey probably would have wandered circles through the apartment all night, obsessively checking under the beds and behind the shower curtains. Instead, she'd stared at the ceiling—perfectly visible with the light on—and prayed over and over for God to hide her from anybody who wanted to kill her.

"You look like you haven't hit the rack in about six weeks."

Casey jumped at the voice, then dropped her hands flat on the desk and leaned back in the chair to look at the face peeking over her cubicle wall.

Staff Sergeant Joel Brenner was the new guy, arriving a couple of months earlier from Fort Sam Houston. Right at six feet tall with dark hair and blue eyes too impossible to be real, he'd caught the attention of every single lady in the office.

Except Casey. Try as she might, she couldn't work up anything other than a feeling of friendship for the man who went out of his way to pay attention to her. He was as nice as he was gorgeous, but nothing made her want to give him a chance. Something inside her must be defective.

Brenner rested his crossed arms on the low wall, his usually laughing eyes grim. "Seriously. What is going on with you, Jordan? You aren't yourself today."

"Didn't sleep well last night." She hadn't told anybody at work what had happened, other than her laptop had been stolen. Even the thought of the uproar if the whole place learned someone had held a gun on one of their own was too much to bear. "You know how it is."

"Getting absorbed by your story?"

"You could say that." In a roundabout, parallel universe kind of way, sure.

"You do realize it's lunchtime?" Brenner slid his hands out to the sides and gripped the top of the cubicle, then leaned back as far as he dared without toppling the wall, surveying the room. "Almost everybody's packed and lit out of here for chow already." He pulled himself in and studied the top of her desk. "Want to go to the Starbucks over by the commissary and grab some real coffee?"

Casey fought to keep from wrinkling her nose. She'd turned him down a hundred times, and a hundred times he'd asked again. Always friendly. Always hopeful. Kind of like a puppy begging for attention…if the puppy was drop-dead gorgeous.

Which might be one of the reasons she couldn't quite get herself to accept a date. A guy who looked like him should never be interested in her. It made no sense. She'd taken the risk with Travis, and look where that had gotten her.

At least today, she had an excuse. "Got an interview scheduled this afternoon, and I have to jet out of here in about three minutes." She glanced at the clock. It was almost noon. Zero hour, when she'd have to decide if she was going to go home to meet Travis or ignore him altogether and go to John's by herself.

Both thoughts left a sour wave in her stomach. There was no good reason for her to want Travis to tag along, but she did nonetheless. Emotional memory must be the same as muscle memory. It was a part of her until she somehow managed to train it out.

"Tomorrow?" Brenner let the question hang and quirked a half grin.

Well, nobody could say he wasn't persistent. "I'm booked. Different guy, same interview."

The grin came on in full force, and it really was a sight to behold. He aimed a finger at her with a wink. "One of these days you'll say yes."

Casey grinned at the good-natured humor in his tone. She wanted to think it was true, that one of these days she'd be able to believe he was interested in her, that she'd be totally herself again and could see another man without coloring him through the lens of Travis Heath. It had been three months, and her world still held the sheen of him, whether she wanted it to or not.

Doubly so with his reappearance.

Forcing a smile, Casey shook her head and reached for the cell phone buzzing on her desk. "Someday could be a mighty long time. I'm thinking you ought to hone in on another target. There are plenty of women around here waiting for you to ask them for coffee, you know."

He shrugged and glanced around the largely empty room, then looked at her, lowering his voice. "I know. But they aren't you." Backing away, he waved and walked away to his cubicle.

Casey watched him go, running her thumb along the smooth case of her cell phone. Why couldn't she tell the guy yes? Even once?

With a sigh Brenner could probably hear from across the room, she flipped her phone over and glanced at the text message hovering on the screen.

I know you're thinking about flaking on me. See you in half an hour.

Travis. Right there was the reason she couldn't tell a guy like Staff Sergeant Brennan yes. Because Travis had wrecked her faith in men.

And he could still read her mind from miles away.

Shoving her phone into the leg pocket of her uniform, she closed her laptop and prepared to do battle not only with Travis, but with her own memories.

Casey twisted her silver ring around her finger and stared out the side window of Travis's pickup, watching the pine trees pass as they drove out of town. The scene was both familiar and strange. She'd been certain she'd never occupy this seat again, yet here she was. Where she shouldn't be. With a guy who was sure to crush her again if given the chance.

This ride-along was nothing like drives together had been in the past, when she'd thought she'd laid claim to some part of his heart. Instead of laughter-fueled conversations, the vehicle seemed to expand with the heavy silence of two familiar strangers loosely bound by memory and what-might-have-been.

Stupid. She should have left from work or bolted from the apartment before he arrived and headed to John's by herself. Should have called him and told him to let it go, she could write her article without his input.

But the truth was, she needed company, even if it meant more time with Travis Heath. After last night, the idea of going anywhere alone brought cold sweat.

In a way, having Travis along for the ride to John's interview was a comfort.

And in a way, it was infinitely more dangerous than any mugger with a gun aimed at her head.

"You're quieter than usual." Travis's voice bounced

in time with the ruts in the dirt driveway that wound through the trees to John's house. "I'm really not used to you not talking."

Well, he should get used to it. Other than *thank you for driving me*—which she'd already said—there was nothing left to talk about. Getting into the whole conversation about why he'd walked away while using the army as a cop-out was too depressing. "I'm more tired than usual."

Not for the first time, Casey wished she had Kristin's boldness. Her friend spoke what she thought and got answers when she needed them. Those attributes made her a good personal trainer, even if it had cost her a few friendships over the years. At least she knew where she stood at all times. Unlike Casey, who could only sit and fume silently instead of launching her hurt into open air.

Casey dug her teeth into her bottom lip as a house appeared in a small clearing. There was a time when she would have reached across the seat and sought Travis's hand for support. When she'd have been the one making the call last night, and he'd have stayed on the phone with her, his voice enough to soothe her fears and let her slip into sleep. But he'd backed off, and where did you run when the person you normally ran to was the one who'd hurt you?

Until yesterday she'd been sure she was done with grieving the dream known as Travis Heath.

Now, well, she'd cut away the bandages to find the wound still raw.

She exhaled loudly as Travis shifted the truck into Park, turning her attention from the man beside her to the house tucked into the woods. John Winslow's house was a small one-story ranch likely built in the late seventies. The wood siding was stained dark, and tall, narrow windows broke the space. There was no grass, only a clearing covered in pine straw from the towering trees dimming the early afternoon light.

The air in the truck cab was stifling. Casey popped open the door and stepped onto the carpet of pine needles. High above, the wind whispered in the trees like quiet voices. The sound crawled along Casey's arms like the echoes of a bad horror movie.

Travis slammed the truck door and came around to meet her, his brow furrowed. "Seems kind of quiet. You sure you got the address right? That this is the time you two agreed on?"

Right now, Casey wasn't sure of anything. She pulled her phone from her hip pocket and checked the text John had sent right after he left the restaurant, then turned the phone so Travis could see. "He should be here." She shoved the phone into her pocket and tilted her head toward the side of the house. "His car's here."

Travis drummed his fingers on the hood of his truck, scanning the roofline and the surrounding trees. "Know the feeling you get when something's hinky? When the hair on the back of your neck stands up?"

"Paranoia because we were mugged last night?" Casey brought on the sass, desperate to deny she felt it, too, an odd sensation that even the air was disturbed.

"Paranoia? Really?" His eyes caught hers and held, the cocky little half smile she used to think was so cute tugging at the corner of his mouth. He broke contact and surveyed the yard. "No. It's too quiet. No birds. No squirrels. Almost like something scared them into hiding."

Casey tilted her head to the side, determined to avoid any more eye contact, and focused on the sounds in the woods around them. Other than the wind talking to itself in the branches above their heads, there was nothing. The silence filtered the day, almost as though every distant noise had to squeeze through the heavy air. "Know what? John told me once he has a dog. Called it a loudmouthed beast who barked at his own shadow. You'd think a vocal dog would react to a truck in the driveway."

The lines on his forehead deepening, Travis turned toward the house and eased his shoulder in front of Casey as though he were taking point on a patrol, his head swiveling from side to side, watching every avenue as they walked the small path to the front door, where the house almost seemed to hold its breath.

Casey wanted to shove him out of the way, but the quiet hung heavier as they drew closer to the door, and the breeze tweaked her imagination, brushing fingers along her neck. She fought a shudder and eased behind Travis, willing to let him take the lead.

The front door stood inside a recessed stoop, the sun's angle cloaking the entry in shadows.

Shadows could be hiding anything, including a man wearing a hoodie and brandishing a pistol. Last night's fear layered over reality, making the warm afternoon instantly sinister. Casey's feet ached to run to the truck and gun the engine until she was on the road, leaving behind only a trail of dirt and pine needles to show she'd been there. Her muscles twitched, fear plucking the strings.

She'd do it, too, tuck tail and shelter in the truck until Travis gave her the all clear, if running didn't mean Travis and John could have a good laugh at her expense. No way would she let that happen.

At the front door, Casey reached around Travis, desperate for a way to remind herself this was broad daylight in the country, not a dark parking lot in town. She rapped her knuckles hard against the wood.

The door swung open with the force of the blow.

Travis stepped aside, shoving Casey squarely behind him. "I knew something was wrong." The muttered words were low but impossible to miss, pumping even more fear into her system.

Fear that had to be misplaced. She was jumpy, wired from having a gun aimed at her. This was silly, the stuff of bad television movies. Real life didn't play out in crime scenes and bloodshed. "Nothing's wrong." She tried to shove ahead of him, swallowing a bout of anxiety, but he stood firm, his shoulder blocking her way.

"Stay behind me." The command in his tone worked, and Travis eased to the side of the door, keeping Casey tucked close to him. He swung the door open with a flat palm. "Winslow? You in there? It's Casey Jordan and Travis Heath."

No sound came from the house.

Casey's skin crawled. From all her interviews with John over the past couple of years, she knew his past experiences had bred a man who would never leave his home unsecured. "What do we do?"

"We go in." Travis shielded her as he crossed the threshold.

This was a dumb idea. What if John was on the phone? Or he'd overslept? "Travis…"

He ignored her.

The front entry opened into the living area, where a

large leather sectional curved around the sunken living room. Narrow floor-to-ceiling windows lined the far wall, the heavy curtains drawn, casting the room in dark shadows. The sole light from the front door fell across the center of the floor.

Casey stayed close to Travis, willing her sight to adjust to the dim interior after the daylight outside. She felt along the wall, hoping they weren't making a huge, embarrassing mistake.

Something like the smell of old pennies tickled her nose, familiar and frightening.

Only one thing smelled like that.

Travis hesitated. He must have caught it, as well. His hand swept along the wall and connected with a switch that flooded the room with light.

On the far left side of the living room, John sat in a kitchen chair, hands lashed behind him, chin hanging to his chest, blood covering the green T-shirt and jeans he'd worn last night and puddling on the floor at his feet.

Casey gasped and stumbled backward, Travis's hold on her hand the only thing that kept her from going down. It was all the borrowed strength she needed. Stomach still roiling, she dug up every reserve she had as Travis's fingers tightened around hers and pulled her forward.

He released her hand and dropped to his knees beside John, searching for a pulse. "He's alive. Barely. Get in the truck, lock yourself in and call 911."

"But…" She'd trained for moments like this, but living a situation where death hung so close was something she wasn't prepared for. She'd been on a large forward operating base during her deployments, not on the front lines, and had seen the wounded from a distance. This much blood, this much pain… Death hovered so close it sucked in all the available air.

With a strangled gasp, John lifted his head and fixed panicked eyes on Casey. His face bore dark bruises, lips swollen and bloodied. His jaw worked, and he made a sound she couldn't understand, a word that simply wouldn't compute past the roaring in her ears.

The brief moment of contact jolted through Casey before John's eyes dulled and he slumped forward, his breath shuddering before it stopped.

# FOUR

Travis pressed the heels of his hands into the metal of his tailgate and forced his shoulders higher, trying to stretch the tension out of his lower back. It felt as though he'd been sitting in the same spot for days, even though emergency vehicles had crowded into John Winslow's small clearing. Now, the quiet that had unnerved him earlier was obliterated by voices, radio calls and squawking emergency scanners.

Paramedics stood near the fire truck, speaking in low tones. On the other side of the vehicles, a small knot of first responders gathered around John's dog, which had been found in the backyard, drugged but coming around. The brown-and-white Brittany spaniel found herself doted on by every person who had a spare minute.

She was a bright spot in a dark scene, but she brought an ache to Travis's chest. The last time he'd had a conversation with John, it had been nearly two years ago, right after John adopted the puppy. Travis hadn't been in the mood to talk. He'd been at the dog park with a buddy, who was adopting Travis's dog before he took off on his last deployment. Travis had introduced the two men, suggested the guy's wife as a veterinarian for John's new puppy, then stayed out of the rest of the conversation. Now, in spite of the fact they'd had their differences along the way, Travis wished he'd been a little bit friendlier. Life was fragile and the end came out of nowhere. He'd learned the lesson well when a hurricane wiped out his small hometown in the Florida Panhandle. He'd seen it when Neil Aiken was there one minute and gone the next and when Kristin's brother had been killed in Iraq. Today, life had fled right in front of him once again.

He grabbed the edge of the tailgate and held tight. Life went too easily, and it couldn't be restored once it was gone.

Exactly like last night. It could have been Casey or him, gone in a moment with a muzzle flash.

Travis dug his teeth into his lower lip. Last night. When the man with a pistol had stolen Casey's laptop.

On the running board of a nearby ambulance, Casey sat stiff, her shoulders a straight line as she stared at the fire truck that had led the charge into the clearing. The police had separated them, probably to keep them from tainting one another's statements, but it was hard to watch her sit silently beside a female EMT who was obviously trying to keep Casey's mind off the sights inside the house.

The paramedics who'd arrived first on the scene had confirmed what Travis already knew. John was gone. That one desperate gasped word—*bet*—had been his last.

Maybe John had owed someone money. He'd heard of pretty rough things happening when compulsive gamblers ran afoul of the wrong people. Maybe the mugging last night had been because someone had seen John with Casey and thought they could get to him through her.

Or maybe it was something else. Whatever the meaning, John had been determined to express it to Casey, even as his life ran out.

Travis couldn't shake the feel of warm blood from his hands, though after the police had cleared him to do so, he'd scrubbed until his skin was raw and red. His attempts at CPR hadn't yielded results. From the looks of John's body, he'd been severely beaten before he died, his face and upper body bearing the evidence of a personal, vindictive anger that would haunt Travis until he drew his own last breath.

One more to add to the list.

Desperate for something else to focus on, he glanced again at Casey across the driveway, her gray pallor a pretty strong indicator she wasn't doing much better than he was.

He prayed she hadn't seen what he had—the laptop on the floor near the couch, the screen and keys splashed with John's blood.

Travis wasn't prepared to stake his life on it, but the vinyl protector over the keyboard looked familiar, exactly like the deep purple cover Casey used on her personal laptop. He'd seen it enough times in the past to get familiar with it, while she typed away as he watched sports on more than a few lazy Sunday afternoons.

He studied her profile, wishing he could explain everything about why those days had died. Coupled with the unlikelihood she'd even listen, his desire to make excuses was futile. He'd ended it. It was over, exactly the way it should be if he was going to move forward with the path God had laid out for him. Besides, there was no reason to start anything now, not when he was about to head out to start selection for the Special Missions Unit that would take him far from here.

Right now, though, with her sitting rigid and traumatized several yards away, all he wanted to do was erase the past three months and let her lean on him. He wanted to give her a silent promise she'd be safe as long as he was around. Somehow he could chase all the monsters away, even as he fought them himself. But he could make such a promise for only a short time.

Still, he was going to stick close for these next two weeks. Surely, he could keep his rational mind about him, if it meant keeping her out of danger. Because if the laptop really was hers, she was tied to John's murder. Either John had stolen her laptop or his killer had, which meant she was close to this. A person who was capable of the kind of brutality that had ended John's life wouldn't hesitate to do the same to Casey. The one thing he couldn't puzzle out was why. What was on her laptop, what did Casey know, that tied all of this together? And why had they left it behind?

One of the officers in the group by the front door broke away and headed for a nearby squad car, his gait familiar. His step stuttered, and a slight grin quirked his mouth. He diverted course and headed toward Travis. "Heath. That's not you, is it?"

The smile didn't fit anything about this day, but battlefield conditions drew out the need for anything to relieve the tension. Travis hopped off the truck with an answering grin. "Brewer. You left behind army green for police blue?"

"Something like that." Marcus Brewer clasped Travis's hand in a tight grip and slapped him on the shoulder. "More like my wife was done after my four years were up. Didn't like the moving once we had the first kid. She decided we ought to settle here so she could be close to her family. It's a long way from Fort Hood, though. Those were good times."

They had been good times, when both of them had been green in the army at their first duty station, heady with new soldier swagger. "And so long ago at this point, I almost can't remember most of it."

Marcus laughed. "You got that right. But one thing I'll never forget. You never had a shortage of very pretty dates." He glanced at Casey, then turned to Travis, his eyebrow arched. "Some things never change."

"Casey's a friend."

"Sure. Right. And I've got eyes that can't see." Marcus hitched his thumbs into his belt. "What are you doing way out here in the middle of a crime scene?"

"John and I served together a few years ago, and Casey was interviewing him for a story. Thought I'd ride along."

"Good thing you did."

Travis bit the inside of his cheek. The comment brought a wave of gratitude he hadn't expected. Last night, the idea to tag along with Casey had been an impulse driven by the image of her under attack and possibly a little misplaced jealousy. Turned out to have been the right call. He didn't want to imagine what might have happened if he hadn't been with her this afternoon.

With a glance over his shoulder at Casey, Marcus leaned closer to Travis, his expression grim. "Look, your friend?" He scratched his cheek, his gaze never leaving Travis's. "Keep an eye on her. She might have trouble headed her way."

The first time Travis had jumped out of an airplane, he'd stood in the door certain his stomach was going to abandon him by bottoming out through his boots. Right now, the same sensation leaped on him with a vengeance.

The laptop. They'd figured out it was Casey's. Somehow, they suspected her.

He tensed for the fight, sending a silent thank-you to God he'd come here with her. If she'd been alone, there would be no alibi. "Number one, Marcus, I did CPR on John. I know..." He swallowed hard against the still-vivid vision. "I saw his injuries. Casey's not capable." He held up a hand to halt whatever Marcus started to say. "Number two, she was with a friend last night, at work this morning and with me this afternoon. She never had a chance to do this."

Marcus thunked a finger against Travis's forehead, the same way he used to do when Travis was getting stupid as a young private. "You done playing defense attorney yet?"

Fine, so he'd jumped the gun. The idea of Casey in handcuffs was a little too much to handle. He gave a stiff nod.

"I doubt someone as tiny as her could have man-handled the victim into that chair. But there's enough evidence to warrant a few extra questions." Arching an eyebrow, Marcus surveyed the area and lowered his voice again. "I saw the report. The two of you were mugged last night. At gunpoint. After she had dinner with the victim. Her laptop was stolen and one matching its description is inside the house next to a dead man. So either this is a crazy coincidence, or she's in some kind of trouble. My man, stay close to her. And if you're a praying person, start. Because you and I both know how rare a coincidence like this would be. That girl over there? She's probably about to be in some real trouble, and the police are the least of her worries."

# FIVE

"Thank you." Casey's hand shook slightly as she took the *grande* green tea from the barista's hand and turned to find a seat. Even now, hours after watching John Winslow take his last breath, hours after watching Travis's frantic attempt to pump life into the man, her nerves still refused to settle. Death overseas was one horrible thing. Death on the home front held a shock value all its own.

Without waiting for Travis, she drifted into the corner of the funky little coffeehouse she usually frequented with Kristin. The familiar warm fragrance of fresh coffee and gourmet chocolates brought a little bit of peace, but Casey wished she had a whole lot more. She sought out the table farthest from the front door, her back to the wall and her peripheral vision capturing the narrow hallway leading to a small enclosed courtyard. Nobody was sneaking up on her. Not in reality and not in her imagination.

Even here, Casey felt exposed, as though everyone from the barista to the solitary man sitting at the table by the front window was watching, waiting for her to…

To what? Breathe normally again? It was certain she

wouldn't be doing that anytime soon. And it was certain shock would dog her deep into the night, keeping her awake when she desperately tried to grasp sleep.

Fighting the chill inside her was futile. Distraction was the only place to hide, so she opened her laptop. Somehow, she couldn't help but think—especially after all the pointed questions the police had asked—John's death lay at her feet because of her article, which meant combing through every note she'd taken.

Travis slid out the bright red chair across from her and moved it to the side so he faced the café at a right angle to her. He put his huge cup of coffee onto the metal table, glancing around the room as he sat. He'd showered at his apartment while Casey ran more updates on her new laptop in the apartment complex's business center. Now a dark blue T-shirt emblazoned with the Denver Broncos logo hugged his chest in place of the gray one he'd worn earlier.

He stretched his arms out to his sides, pulling his T-shirt tight across his chest. "This place is so tiny, I think I could touch both walls with my fingertips."

Casey smiled, unable to hold on to her anger at him in view of all they'd witnessed today. Bless Travis. This was what she needed. Normalcy. Conversation devoid of dead men and beatings.

She shuddered and pushed the laptop aside, forcing herself to focus on the bright yellow wall covered with vintage concert posters. "You've never been here?"

"I've rarely been downtown. No reason to, really. It's…cute."

"You say that like it's a bad thing."

"Not bad. Just cute." He flashed her a grin that telegraphed how hard he was trying to make everything all better and took a sip of his drink. "Coffee's good."

"It is." Mimicking his gesture, she sipped the green tea and grimaced. She never drank the stuff. It tasted too much like fresh-cut grass smelled. Today, though, the thought of her usual cherry-mocha coffee had given her stomach pause. "Thanks for understanding I wasn't ready to go home." Although coffee with Travis Heath was pretty low on her list of ought-to-dos, it was a better alternative than her empty apartment without a way to distract herself from the visions in her head.

Travis started to say something, then lifted his cup and tipped it toward her in a salute instead.

"What?"

One eyebrow arched at her in innocent question.

Casey wasn't buying the routine. "What were you about to say?"

Setting the cup on the table, Travis took his time getting it positioned. "You're not the only one who needed company, so don't go thinking you're weak. If you want the truth, I ought to be thanking you for suggesting this place." He swung out his arm to encompass the rock-and-roll decor. "Even if I feel like I need sunglasses indoors."

A genuine smile tugged at the corner of Casey's mouth. Nothing about him had changed. Not the way he read her every thought. Not the hair that was never as short as the army said it should be. And not the smile that quirked his lips, an indication of the humor crackling through every situation.

The ripple inside her stomach this time had nothing to do with what she'd seen during the morning, but it was equally dangerous. No matter what she felt,

Travis represented everything she didn't want out of life. It took a lot of concentration to force her words out evenly. "Go ahead. Try to feel dark in here. Can't be done. I come here as often as I can."

"You come here a lot? Since when? Pretty sure I'd never be able to forget you bringing me here." He shifted to look at something by the front door, almost like he knew he might have gone too far.

Except it didn't feel like too far. And it didn't feel like what Casey had feared bringing up the past would. Until the very last second of their relationship, he had never made her feel anything other than safe and happy. And then…nothing. Sitting with Travis shouldn't be like slipping on an old shoe. Feeling comfortable around him was easy and dangerous, asking to walk right into the same emotions that had let him hurt her before, even if the pain had likely saved them both a lot more trouble in the long run.

But sitting here did bring comfort. Peace. Today, she needed comfort more than she needed to guard her heart.

She shrugged off his comment. "It's more of a me and Kristin thing. Girl time. I never thought about bringing you. It's not really your kind of place, is it?"

His eyes narrowed, never leaving hers, the intensity of his stare amping the tremor in her stomach. "A lot of things aren't me." He leaned closer, forearms resting on the table. "I know the timing stinks, but there's something I—"

"Travis?" A woman's voice whipped across the coffeehouse and snapped into the moment.

He trailed off, his jaw jutting forward. Catching

himself, he relaxed his expression and turned toward the front of the shop and the voice.

Casey wanted to be relieved that whatever serious topic he'd been about to delve into had been derailed, but something in her strained toward him, pushing against her skin. It was probably good they'd been interrupted, because wherever he was headed, she didn't need to follow.

A tall woman, blond hair flowing in thick waves to her shoulders, squeezed past a customer in the narrow space by the counter and headed toward them. She was smiling directly at Travis.

It felt like a punch to the throat.

A double punch when Travis stood and the woman threw her arms around his neck like he was her long-lost best friend.

She was as gorgeous as they came. The slim jeans she wore with high-heeled sandals made her look leggier than she already was. And she'd probably been schooled in how to apply makeup to achieve a look both natural and flawless.

Casey sat on her hands to keep from reaching up to check how wild the wind had made her own short blond hair, which wouldn't shine like that even if she dumped olive oil on it. She probably looked as though she'd been spit out of a hot dryer halfway through the cycle. No competition here.

"Meredith." Travis's shoulders squared more than usual, and he watched the front of the shop warily as though he expected a gunman to burst through the door at any second. "Is Phil with you?"

For the barest second, the other woman's expression

dropped, but she caught herself and smiled, waving a hand behind her. "Parking the car."

"And how's Gus?"

She grinned, her smile truly genuine for the first time, the joy radiant. "Gus is great. He's a good dog, Travis. You should come by and see him. Phil would love if you visited."

"It's too hard to see him." A shadow ghosted Travis's face then vanished, almost as though regret winged by and he'd mentally swatted it away.

He didn't retake his seat but stood by the table. He took a step away from Meredith and nodded toward Casey. "Meredith, this is Casey Jordan. Casey, this is Meredith Ingram. She and her husband, Phil, adopted my dog Gus. She was Gus's vet, and when it came time for this last deployment, they took him in. It's better for him to have a stable home with them than to watch me leave every time the army needs me elsewhere."

"Adopted your dog? There's so much more to…" She pivoted her entire body toward Casey, surveying her with the kind of interest usually reserved for famous athletes or rock stars. "Wait a second. Casey Jordan?" She glanced over her shoulder at Travis. "*The* Casey Jordan?"

Before Travis could speak, a deeper voice intruded. "My turn to say hello to the prodigal." A man Casey hadn't noticed reached around the woman to clasp Travis's shoulder. He was as tall as Travis and as well built, too, his biceps peeking out the sleeves of a red polo shirt that sported an NC State University logo on the right chest. Deep brown eyes crinkled with a smile. "How long's it been, man? Three months?"

*Three months.* Casey's jaw slackened. Whoever

these people were, they were close to Travis, yet they hadn't seen him in three months. The same time he'd walked away from her.

The timing was too perfect to be a coincidence.

She shoved her chair from the table with a scrape on the concrete floor. This was a chance to edge closer to the truth. Smiling, she extended her hand to the woman. "Yes, I'm Casey Jordan."

Travis stared, wearing one of those slightly guilty expressions, as though he'd gotten caught at something Casey couldn't quite puzzle out. The wheels turning in his head were practically audible.

"So good to finally meet you. This is my husband, Phil." The woman took Casey's hand warmly, but then her grip tightened and she pulled Casey toward her, her eyebrow arching in amusement. Her smile widened and she glanced at Travis as she wrapped her other hand around Casey's. "Do tell, Travis. I thought the two of you had split."

Casey arched her own eyebrow at Travis and smiled. Rarely did he get rattled, but he was right now. This could be interesting and definitely better than everything else they could find to discuss this afternoon.

*Yes, Travis. Do tell.*

So this was what it felt like to be pinned to the wall.

The moment was surreal, as though the past three months hadn't happened and he'd somehow time warped into his old life, with Casey by his side and Meredith and Phil as his friends.

It was one thing to run into Meredith. She was merely Phil's wife, not a key player in everything that had happened three months ago.

But Phil? Phil was another story. One he definitely didn't want brought up in front of Casey. After the way the other man had acted the night Travis and Casey had split, he couldn't even look at the friend who had once walked with him through some of the hardest moments in his life.

But the way Meredith and Casey were both watching him now, they expected him to start talking.

He cracked a smile and crossed his arms, digging his fingernails into his palms. He'd honestly never expected to make this introduction. "Nothing to tell. Meredith and Phil, and yes, this is Casey."

"Just Casey? Not *my friend* Casey? My *acquaintance* Casey?"

Man, Meredith was pushy. She couldn't let this go? Couldn't stand there like her husband and be silent? No, she couldn't. He'd known her since high school in Florida. Even then, she was a talker driven by the need to know everything. Meeting Phil at North Carolina State and settling into marriage with him hadn't dimmed her nosiness.

Casey's cheeks reddened, and she looked at the table as she extracted her hand from Meredith's. "Some of Travis's former teammates are helping me with an article I'm writing."

True, but he hated the way her voice quieted, like she wasn't quite worthy of being here unless there was a practical reason. He hazarded a glance at Phil, who was watching Casey with an expression Travis couldn't read.

Phil caught Travis looking and scratched his chin, his fingers crisscrossed with fresh scratches and bruises. "I remember Travis saying you were with Public Affairs. What's this story on?"

"Someone I interviewed a while back gave me an idea for something else to chase, so I'm pursuing some leads." Casey's smile didn't quite reach her eyes as she tilted her head and let her gaze fall to Phil's fingers. "You look like something chewed you up there."

Phil glanced at his hand with a rueful grin. "*Chewed* is the perfect word. Meredith had a dog turn rowdy at the kennel early this morning, and I was doing my best to be a good husband."

"I told you to let Dylan handle it, but no, you had to go over there when he called." Meredith winked at Casey with a knowing look. "Somehow, they always think we need them to rush in and save us. I'm pretty sure Travis has been the same way since high school."

This was all way too cute and fluffy. With his patience stretched thin by the morning's pain and his mind shouting memories of Phil's complete betrayal, this conversation was growing unbearable.

Phil had been Travis's ear when he had been trying to work out whether he'd done the right thing by leaving Casey. It had been during one of those discussions when Travis had found himself sitting in Phil's backyard about to tip back the beer that would set him on a downward spiral.

The beer Phil had handed him, knowing how hard Travis had struggled to keep himself off a dangerous road. The worst was the additional insinuation. *And if the beer doesn't work, we'll move on to something stronger.*

That was the real reason it had been three months since Meredith and Phil had seen him. Because for all the good advice he'd dished out, Phil's beer-around-a-bonfire solution for all negative feelings was bad news for Travis's self-discipline. Defiance rose in Travis and he stood taller, silently commanding the other man to back off.

Swallowing hard, Travis held out his hand to his former friend. "It's good to see you and I hate to cut this short, but Casey and I were in the middle of some work and we need to get to it."

Phil stared at his extended hand, something like annoyance playing across his face before he took it. "We'll get together one day and have lunch. And, hey, you should at least come out and see the dog. He'd like a visit, I'm sure."

"Maybe." But he doubted it. Leaving the Australian shepherd behind had been harder than he'd expected, and time with the Ingrams led to nothing but trouble.

Phil nodded to Casey. "It's nice to meet you."

Over his shoulder, Meredith tilted her head, probably thrown sideways by the abrupt end to the conversation. "Sure. We should get going or we'll miss the matinee at the Cameo." She flashed a quick smile as her husband turned and ushered her to the narrow space by the main counter.

Casey sat and pulled her laptop close again. "She's pretty."

There was a hint of resignation in the way Casey said it, and it almost drove Travis to say something he shouldn't. Meredith was all smoke and mirrors, and of all the women he'd ever seen, Casey topped the list.

None of their history was important, but he felt the deep need to let Casey know Meredith had never been anything more than a friend. "Meredith and I were in some of the same classes, yes. I didn't really get to know her until I moved here and needed a vet for Gus. My parents knew hers, told me when she got married, and I recognized her name when I was searching." With a deep sigh of resignation, he pointed at the laptop she'd squared in front of her on the table. "Have you found anything?"

"I've glanced through some notes, but I can't imagine what would be worth killing a man over."

"You still think this has to do with your article?" She'd said as much on the ride from John's house, blaming herself somehow for his death. A death Travis still couldn't scrub off his hands, no matter how often he washed them or ran them along the sides of his jeans. He wrapped his fingers around the coffee cup, wishing it was hot enough to burn away the sensation that lingered on his skin.

"I don't know. It's not like anything I'm writing is going to rock anybody's world. It's a follow-up piece. Unless there's classified info somebody's afraid I'll uncover, there's nothing new to see here."

"Nothing about the mission was ever classified. We were working with Border Patrol, and we stumbled on a group smuggling drugs in from Mexico. It was a big deal because of the ramifications of the takedown. Otherwise, it was pretty routine."

"Then maybe we were mugged last night and John's coincidentally dead today." She tapped her thumb on the keyboard for a long moment, staring at the screen before she looked up. "Except I saw my laptop by John's couch. And the police had plenty of questions about that. Somehow, all of this is connected."

The way her face paled, Travis thought she was

going to bolt from the table. He wanted to slide his chair over and wrap his arms around her for no other reason than to hold her up in the middle of this craziness. He'd hoped—along with Marcus—she hadn't seen the laptop. But his hope was gone, and she was hurting.

There was nothing he could do about it. Travis dropped his hands to his thighs and balled his fists to keep from touching her. When he'd walked out on her, he'd forfeited every right to be her hero. Now, all he could do was sit in his place and make sure he stayed between her and danger, in a way that didn't say he cared.

Because he couldn't.

It took a second, but Casey stiffened her shoulders and lifted her head, focused on one of the autographed posters across the room. "If somebody took my laptop and went after someone I was interviewing, they must think he told me something."

"Or they thought hurting you would hurt John."

Casey barked a harsh laugh. "Um, no. Nobody wants me bad enough to beat a man to death to get to me. Try again. Even you—" She stuttered to a stop, her cheeks flashing red as she turned her attention to the screen of the laptop. "No. All of this has to be something about the mission you guys were on."

Travis wanted to find a way to punch himself in the face. He was the jerk. He was the one who'd wounded her, who'd made her feel like she wasn't worth his time, all because he'd been too chicken to tell her the truth. "I need to explain—"

"No. You don't. We're done. And if all of this wasn't

happening now, there wouldn't be any reason for you to even be here."

He started to try again, but he knew she wouldn't hear him. He sat stone still, letting her take the lead, wishing he could make her understand but waiting to see which direction she'd go.

"I'm moving forward with the story. Whoever came at us last night wanted my laptop. He asked for it first, then added your wallet as an afterthought. All my notes and my contact info are on there. The mission wasn't classified, but this could be about revenge, somebody from the cartel you disrupted coming at you guys. If somebody wanted to get to you—"

"Then they would have taken a shot at me last night."

"Unless they didn't realize who you were."

"Or you're wrong." Couldn't she see she was in danger? Travis would give his right arm for him to be the target instead of her. He couldn't imagine losing her, even though she was no longer his to lose.

She ignored him. "I meet another soldier from your former team, Deacon Lewis, tomorrow at noon. I called him from work this morning and I didn't put it in my online calendar, so if John's killer accessed my devices, he wouldn't have any way of knowing. If this is revenge, Deacon should be safe."

"You have no proof this is revenge. So far, the sole link you have to my mission is your story and John. Nobody's come at me. This could be about something completely different, something we haven't even considered."

"But what if you're wrong?" She closed the lid on her laptop and stared at her fingers as she fidgeted with the cover. "And what if you're next?"

# SIX

*What if you're next?*

Casey's question hung in the air between them, the words so heavy they almost left an imprint in the stillness over the table. Last night, his attention had been on Casey. This afternoon, on the futile attempt at saving John and now on putting puzzle pieces together. The idea of being in danger was as remote as a combat outpost on the other side of the world.

But it made the hairs on the back of his neck come to full attention.

It was hard not to turn around and make sure no one was surveilling him…or aiming a gun at the back of his head.

Today was the worst day for paranoia. The perception of hidden eyes watching him crawled all the way down his spine and into his knees. He'd battled hard to overcome the fear that ate at him after Aiken died. Then, on his last deployment, a sniper's shot had left Kristin's brother dead. It had taken months for Travis to stop believing there was a bullet headed for him. The sensation rushed in again, surging his mind and body into overdrive.

He scrubbed the back of his neck and tried not to sound strangled. "Nobody's trying to take me out. Co-incidences are a rarity—"

"Something I've heard you say more than once."

"But your thread is tenuous. The timing's off if somebody's out for revenge. The mission was years ago. The story's wide open for anybody to read if they bother to search the internet. Finding us before now would have been easy." Really, was he saying it to convince her, or to convince himself?

Either way, Casey didn't look convinced. She gently pushed her laptop to the center of the table, then pressed her palms against her eyes. "I don't know what to think anymore. I'm too—"

"Drained?" She looked it.

Her sun-kissed cheeks were pale and the delicate skin beneath her eyes shadowed when she dropped her hands to the table. "Maybe it's time to go home and face my empty apartment and try to catch some sleep." She shoved her chair away from the table, the scrape of metal on concrete harsh on Travis's frayed nerves.

*I'll crash on your couch if it helps.* The words nearly leaped out before Travis could wrestle them down. Even with the tenuous situation they were facing, such an offer overstepped reasonable bounds. But if it came to it, there was nothing to stop him from bunking in his truck with a straight-line view of her door.

Although Casey had always had an uncanny knack for knowing what he was thinking, she was off her game today. Good thing, or she'd reach across the table and smack him.

She went right on talking as she gathered the laptop's

power cord. "You were on the phone with me late last night, so you probably ought to catch some rest, as well."

Yep. She had no idea what was on his mind. Travis couldn't help but grin as he watched her shove her laptop and cord into a backpack.

On the way out, Casey waved at the barista and promised to see her in a couple of days, threading her way past a man a couple of inches shorter than her, who was ordering at the narrow space by the counter.

The man didn't leave much room for Casey to squeeze past, watching her carefully as she tucked her backpack closer and edged by with a quiet "Excuse me."

Travis totally got it. Casey was gorgeous, but the guy didn't need to be eyeballing her like she was a cookie in the pastry case. He brushed the man's back as he passed, a subtle signal to turn his attention elsewhere.

The guy cast Travis a hostile glare, almost said something, then curled his lip with disgust and turned to the barista again.

Whatever. Travis had bigger fish to fry than a guy with no manners. At least he'd managed to stop the dude from leering after Casey where she waited, oblivious to the scrutiny, holding the door open for him in a way that said she was ready to get moving now that she'd decided to face her fears.

Slipping on his sunglasses even though trees and buildings shaded the sidewalk, Travis glanced up and down the street. He still couldn't shake the prickly feeling of being watched. He scanned the sidewalk and looked over his shoulder. At least it wasn't the coffee shop patron, who'd vanished from the counter to some other spot in the store.

Travis flipped a half salute to the barista and let the door slip shut.

He needed to get over himself. Maybe go for a long run—which he hated—or pack it in and drive to the beach and back to clear his head of the morning, his hands of the sensation of trying to pump life into John's battered body and failing miserably.

If he and Casey were still together, he'd have suggested a quick run to the coast, a dinner of sandwiches and soda while they dug their toes in the sand, then return by midnight. It was half on his tongue to ask, but like bunking on her couch, it probably wasn't a smart idea.

"You look like you're plotting something." Casey had stopped at the edge of the brick sidewalk and was eyeballing him like she really could read his thoughts.

That would be scary.

He looked both ways, waiting for a break in the Friday evening line of cars easing their way along the brick-paved street. "Me? Plotting? Not at all."

An older Nissan 280ZX stopped half a block away and flashed its lights.

Travis and Casey both threw a wave of thanks and stepped into the street, aiming for Travis's truck on the other side.

A sudden squeal tore the air.

Casey froze.

Travis whipped his head toward the sound, trying to place it.

Adrenaline crashed through him in a lightning jolt of pain as the Nissan roared straight for them.

* * *

It was a nightmare. One of those nightmares where Casey wanted to run, but her body was paralyzed, struck by lightning as the friendly car that had stopped to let them cross launched into a bullet aimed straight for them. People running, screaming, the cars screeching to a halt across the street… Everything went into super slow motion as her reflexes locked her feet to the bricks of the pavement.

And then a force slung her sideways and backward. Her shoulder smashed into something hard, the air driven from her lungs as she slid to the pavement and the world spun faster, coming into focus as the sound of the engine grew deafening, the car so close the wind flung her hair as the vehicle roared past.

"Travis!" The shout tore from her throat. Had he been hit? Ignoring the pain in her side and the crowd rushing toward her, she rolled to her knees and slung her backpack to the ground.

Travis knelt beside her, his palms warm on either side of her face. "Case, look at me. We're okay."

She latched on to blue eyes she'd been avoiding since yesterday. "You're not hurt?"

"Banged my knee on the sidewalk." His voice was low, meant only for her, a strange out-of-context sound in the wave of adrenaline rising inside her.

They'd almost been mowed down by a car. Purposely. The shaking started in her core and radiated outward.

"Case…" Travis's hands fell away as someone in dark clothes—a policeman maybe?—eased her back from Travis to sit against the car she'd smashed into, asking her questions she answered mechanically through a fog of fear and adrenaline.

Everything happened too fast. An ambulance, a blanket around her shoulders, more questions. Had she hit her head? Should she be transported to the hospital?

"No." The fog blew away with the final question. "No." She didn't want to go anywhere but wherever Travis was. Resolve washed over her, ebbing the fear. She shoved off the blanket around her shoulders and tried to push herself from the ground.

"Ma'am." The paramedic's voice was a command as he eased her to the street. "Sit down. I really think you—"

"I'll sign whatever you want, but I'm not going to the hospital. I didn't hit my head. I can move my shoulder." She rotated her arm, forcing herself not to wince at the forming bruise.

"A shock considering how hard you hit that parked car. Witnesses said the guy you were with grabbed your backpack and jerked you out of the way."

Travis. "Is he still here? Take me to him."

The young man eyed her, judging her resolve, then muttered, "Stubborn as the other one."

*The other one.* "Where is he?"

The paramedic tipped his head to something behind her as he folded the blanket Casey had dropped. "Talking to the police. Well, trying to get over here, but they won't let him until we clear you." Holding a hand out, he helped ease her up.

The officer who stood in front of Travis glanced over his shoulder then moved out of her way. He looked familiar, maybe one of the policemen from John's house.

John's death. Their mugging. The car…

Without caring one bit what it might mean, she walked straight into Travis's outstretched arms.

He held her tight against him, his arms firm around her waist. "Casey." Her name was almost a sigh of relief.

The same sound her heart had made when she saw him standing on his own, uninjured. Right now, she'd be content to stay here forever.

When her legs stopped shaking, she eased away from him and looked at his face, checking for injuries.

He looked at her as though he wanted to draw her to him again. "You're fine? Really? I tried to get to you and they kept telling me to—"

"I am." The words cracked with an emotion she couldn't begin to define. Her fingers ached to run across his face, to trace down his arms, to know with solid confirmation that she hadn't lost him. "You're okay?"

"Perfect." Travis scanned Casey's face, asking silent questions she didn't want to answer before the straight line of his shoulders eased. He glanced from her to the officer beside him and lowered his voice. "This cop here's a real stickler for the rules."

The officer standing beside Travis straightened and bit back a smile. "You keep it up, Heath. I'll start telling stories about the times you couldn't have cared less about the rules."

"Don't even think about it." Travis finally relaxed. "Casey, this is an old buddy of mine, Marcus Brewer. Marcus, this is Casey Jordan."

"Not sure I like the term 'old,' but, hey, whatever works." Marcus leaned around Travis and extended his hand. "Nice to meet you, Casey Jordan. Saw you earlier at our other crime scene, but it didn't seem like the time for an introduction. Seems like you've had your fair share of trouble the past couple of days."

His hand was smooth in hers, his grip strong and reassuring. While his stance invited friendship and showed a little bit of concern, there was no need to let a stranger see how rattled she was. Casey slipped the mask into place that kept people from giving her sympathy, became the soldier who could handle anything. "I've had more excitement than I'm used to, for sure. Weren't you at John Winslow's house earlier today?"

"I was." His head tilted slightly as he withdrew his hand, almost like he'd asked himself a silent question. "I was going to ask how you're doing, but you seem to be handling things pretty well."

She wasn't. At all. If she let her true, honest self loose right now, she'd curl up in the middle of the sidewalk like an armadillo and take Travis with her, trying to deflect any more arrows fired their way.

She didn't have to look directly at Travis to know he was still watching her, trying to read if she was really doing as well as she claimed to be. Hopefully, he was out of practice. The last thing she wanted was for him to realize she was about to crumble.

# SEVEN

Shifting the truck into Park, Travis turned to look at Casey for the first time since they'd left downtown.

She didn't move, simply stared out the front windshield as though she hadn't noticed they'd arrived at her apartment.

She'd put on some crazy brave face in front of Marcus, but the act couldn't be real. Even Marcus had sent him a cocked eyebrow, a sure indicator he wasn't buying Casey's routine either.

Sure, they'd been apart almost longer than they'd dated, but still... He knew Casey, and he knew when she was lying. The woman was strong, but nobody could stand under what she'd endured in less than twenty-four hours. There had to be a breaking point. If Travis was going to be honest, he was barely holding it all in check himself.

His own emotional high-wire act made him worry about Casey more. She'd always had a need to appear stronger than she was, almost as though asking for help made her weak. Maybe it had to do with something in her childhood. Maybe it had to do with being a female in the army. Travis had never been able to figure it out, and he'd been cracking the shell around her when he realized he had to leave her. Still, he knew when she was hiding.

The straight posture, the set of her jaw, the way she held her hands casually at ease on top of her thighs… Everything said she was holding in major emotions and trying to act as though she wasn't.

The question was whether to call her on it or to let her keep right on lying to him and maybe even to herself.

As though someone had flipped a switch, Casey swung into motion, leaning forward to haul her backpack onto her lap. "Thanks for going with me today."

"Any time." Surprisingly, he meant it. In spite of the insanity, something about being with her reminded him of what he'd seen in her the very first day, when she'd followed Kristin into Lucas's house and walked seamlessly into his life. Something in her quieted him, made him feel like he could take on anything, even cars careening out of control.

And that was a recipe for disaster.

Getting involved with her again would make it harder to walk away when he had to. And he already knew, if he was going to follow the path God had laid out for him, he'd have to.

He shut his eyes and reveled in the nothingness, wishing a map would appear in the darkness and show him a clear path for his life. God didn't work that way. He'd already told Travis what to do, whether he liked it or not.

He blinked and stared at the front of Casey's apartment building, where the shadows were long and deep in the moments before sunset. With the darkness not yet settled, the exterior lights had yet to come on, leaving the breezeway to her apartment cloaked in semidarkness. Clicking his seat belt to release it, he turned to Casey and prepared for battle. "I'm going in with you to make sure everything's safe."

"Seriously?" All the pent-up emotion she'd been holding in unleashed in his direction, a volcanic eruption of words. "No. Travis, you don't get it at all. I'm fine. I'm safe. Nobody's after me. It's you. Your team. Your mission. This evening did nothing but prove it."

He wanted to argue. The words tried to pound their way out, but he couldn't do it. She was right. There was no longer a way to deny he was somehow tangled in this.

But so was she. Letting her think differently was dangerous. "Not even the police know who the target was today. It could have been both of us."

"John's dead. You were on a mission together, and they tried to take you out."

"You talked to Deacon this afternoon and he's fine."

She dropped her head against the truck seat, fingering the strap on her backpack. "I'm not conceding. I know nothing of value. Nothing. You said it yourself earlier. What I know is what your guys have told me, and it's readily available public information. There has to be something more. Either that, or the laptop really is a very strange coincidence. But, Travis, honestly. It looks like somebody has your former team in the crosshairs, and I'm worried about you." Her hand eased across the truck seat and found his wrist, tentative, as though she was afraid he'd bolt.

She shouldn't worry he was a flight risk. As much as he should let her walk away, he couldn't do it. The warmth of her touch was enough to cement that firmly. He stared at her fingers, light on the bare skin of his wrist, then slid his gaze up her arm until he caught her eyes, those gray eyes he still saw every night as he tried to fall asleep. His voice had better not betray him now. "You're worried about me? Deacon was on my team, too, and I don't see you hovering over him like you feel…"

The world seemed to pause. He was holding his breath, and he was pretty sure she was holding hers, as well.

The urge to meet her halfway and press his lips to hers like he had so many times before in this very front seat in this very parking spot was overwhelming. He wanted to wipe away the obligations of his calling, forget either one of them might not survive the next explosion. All he wanted was Casey in his life, making him feel as though nothing else in the world really mattered.

His gaze drifted to her mouth. He could kiss her right now. He could beg her to forgive him for being an idiot and ask her for another chance to have everything he'd ever truly wanted.

As though she could read his thoughts, Casey's head jerked. Her fingers stiffened, and her chin rose as she broke contact, then shoved the truck door open without a break in the action. "Thanks for the ride, Travis. And for being there this morning when…" She dug her teeth into her lower lip, staring at the radio. "You know what? I've got this. Thanks again." She slammed the door so hard the truck rocked and the thud echoed off the building.

Travis wanted to pound his forehead against the steering wheel. Stupid. He'd pushed her places he had no business pushing her. He'd given in to momentary selfishness, put his needs over hers because she made him feel ten feet taller than he was. He'd forgotten why he was here—not to follow his heart but to ~~follow~~ make right the mistakes he'd made years before.

Still, he couldn't stop himself from following her to her door. If he drove away and she disappeared—or worse—because he'd sped off like a man rejected, he'd never be able to face himself.

The air in the breezeway was still and heavy, as though it mocked Travis's concern. Casey was shoving her key into the dead bolt when he caught her, but she stopped after she twisted the lock. "I said thank you and goodbye. So...goodbye."

In any other situation, he'd have laughed. She sounded so much like a character in one of those cheesy chick flicks. But the situation wasn't funny, and his standing beside her had nothing to do with romance.

When she tugged the key from the lock, he reached around and pushed the door open, edging in before she could. If there was a bullet or a knife, he'd be the one to take it, not her.

"You've lost your mind." Casey planted her palms against his back and shoved, but Travis refused to give. He scanned the living room and kitchen. Nothing was out of place. Even the French doors leading to the second-story balcony were tightly shut.

Maybe he was paranoid.

Casey pushed past him. "Nobody's after me. And nobody's..." She stopped, scanning the room as though she saw something he didn't.

"What?" Every fight reaction he'd trained over the years stood at attention, ready to defend.

Ready to defend not only himself, but the woman in front of him, who still somehow managed to work her way under his skin.

"I don't know." She shook her head, thankfully oblivious to his thoughts. "It feels like…" Casey dropped her backpack to the hardwood entry and eased onto the carpet, scanning the room. "It feels like when run your hand through the water in a swimming pool and, before it washes in, there's the track you left behind."

Travis knew the sensation too well. It was the same one he'd had before Aiken had been killed. The same one he should have listened to then.

Well, he was listening today.

Before Casey could protest, Travis grabbed her shoulder, shoving her behind him. "Get out. Get in my truck and lock the doors."

"Will you stop?" Ducking under his arm, she charged into the middle of the living room, the action driving Travis's instincts into overdrive.

He almost made a running dive to push her to safety. She was going to get herself killed if somebody really was in the apartment. Instead, he balled his fists and strode in after her.

Throwing her arms out to the sides, Casey turned slowly. "If somebody was in here, they'd have been on us the instant we came through the door. If anybody was in my apartment, they're gone now. Let's attribute this to me being jumpy and move on."

"I'm still checking your closets."

To his surprise, she didn't argue, simply nodded and pointed to the door leading to the guest room she also used as her office.

Something in her demeanor had changed, as though she were quitting. Travis didn't have time to puzzle out why, not until he knew nobody lurked behind a curtain ready to do to her what someone had done to John.

The very idea sent fire through him. Nobody got to lay a hand on Casey. The thought of her in terror and pain…

He'd die before he let it happen. Would make a fool of himself sleeping in a sleeping bag against her front door. But he wouldn't let anyone harm the woman he'd once loved.

Flipping on the bedroom light, he surveyed the room, stopping at her desk.

Drawers hung open, contents scattered across the floor. A monitor lay on its face, cables leading to no-where. Two telltale dust-free squares shouted an in-dictment.

Her computer and her external drive were gone.

Frustrated with her brain's inability to stay in the zone, Casey stalked into Kristin's kitchen, where her friend was busy fussing with two huge jars. Casey slammed her well-worn sudoku book on the granite counter. Usually, focusing on numbers helped her let go of the day's stress and relax. Tonight, she'd made such a mess she wasn't even sure if two plus two really did equal four anymore.

Kristin glanced up with an arched eyebrow, then wrinkled her forehead as she studied a jar filled with what looked like tea. "Stress getting to you?"

"I wish." Every time Casey had picked up her pencil to write, the slight tremor in her hand had frustrated her. She could shove and push and pack down the violent visions in her mind, but they refused to stay locked away. She was afraid of what would happen when she closed her eyes to sleep tonight. Even more afraid of turning off the lights and letting her mind drift.

And the way her head was all twisted up, she'd nearly forgotten the past few months and fallen into what she used to have with Travis. For her, nothing had changed. Time hadn't healed her heart, it had only buried what she felt for Travis under a layer of ice he melted a little bit more every time he looked at her.

Casey dug her bare toes into the tile floor and watched Kristin slide another jar closer to the first one. She was desperate for distraction, to stop seeing the car spewing tire smoke as it gunned for them. Her grip tightened on the pencil she still held until the wood dug into the side of her finger. She had to relax. Both she and Travis were safe for now.

Rolling the pencil onto the counter, she flexed her fingers then glanced around the kitchen of Kristin's small house in Haymount, giving herself permission to let go. Here there was more peace than she'd been able to find in her apartment. As much as she'd insisted the night before a babysitter was the last thing she needed, tonight she knew... Somebody else on vigil was a pretty good thing.

She wrinkled her nose and looked at Kristin, who was studying the contents of the second jar with a strange look on her face. "What exactly are you doing?"

"Slowly turning into a health-food nut." Kristin didn't turn, but simply tilted the jar slightly, staring at something floating on top of about an inch of dark liquid inside.

Well, this was definitely less stressful than Travis's

reappearance or someone trying to kill them. Casey edged closer and peeked into the jar. Near the bottom, a slimy disk like a smashed jellyfish floated. She edged away and stared at her best friend. "Please, please, please tell me you aren't going to eat whatever that is."

"I'm not."

Casey puffed out a breath. "Good."

"I'm going to drink it."

"Yuck. What on earth is it? And why would you want to drink something that looked like it came from the bottom of the ocean?"

Laughing, Kristin reached in and chased the offending object around the glass before she grasped it and pulled it out, then slipped it onto the top of the liquid in the other jar. "It's as squishy as it looks." She shuddered and wiped her hands on a paper towel. "It's eventually going to be kombucha tea. But I'm really not sure this is something I want to put a lot of time into yet." Slipping a paper towel over the mouth of the jar, she secured it with a rubber band, then slid it to the back of the counter. "Ask me in a few days how it goes."

"How about I ask Lucas instead?"

"He'll call me a granola bar." With a grin, Kristin rinsed her hands then leaned against the counter and reached for an orange. She poked her thumb into the peel, then licked a stray rivulet of orange juice from her finger, her eyes gleaming. "And then he'll ask me again if I'm serious when I say I'm not wearing a dress to our wedding."

"Oh, you're wearing a dress."

"I know, but messing with Lucas and his aunt is too much fun. I think she's half-convinced I'm going to show up in yoga pants and a running shirt. And I can't say I've done much to ease those fears for her."

Casey laughed and jumped up to sit on the counter, shutting her eyes and reveling in the camaraderie as she leaned her head against the cabinet. Yes. She'd been right. It felt good to talk about anything other than the current chaos in her life. "We should do this more often. I forgot what girl time looks like."

"I keep calling, and you keep making excuses."

There was no denying it. Spending time with Kristin had been too much, had brought too many memories of double dates and nights hanging out together as two happy couples. Becoming the third wheel to Kristin and Lucas sounded like zero fun. "Busy."

"Sure." Kristin looked like she was going to say something else, then gave a crooked smile. "But we should hang out more. It might keep Lucas from talking about the wedding. He's a girl when it comes to this."

Casey smiled, even though she didn't really want to. If Lucas joined them, it meant Travis would probably tag along, particularly with his current insistence on watching out for her.

"That man's as stubborn as they come."

"Lucas? He's been pretty flexible about the whole wedding thing."

Oops. She hadn't meant to speak the thought out loud. With a sigh, Casey opened her eyes and stared at the ceiling, where a small crack from the settling of the old house snaked its way beside the tops of the dark wood cabinets. "Not Lucas."

"Travis." A shuffle and a scraping sound said Kristin had dropped into a kitchen chair and was sitting in her customary listening position, elbows on her knees.

Casey peeked. Sure enough, her friend sat exactly like she'd thought, toying with the edges of the paper towel on which her orange slices rested. Kristin ate oranges constantly. It was a wonder the acid hadn't melted her teeth and trashed her stomach.

Kristin popped another orange slice into her mouth and chewed slowly, staring at the refrigerator. "I know you don't want to talk about why you're spending the night here tonight. I totally get it. Been there, done that." The year before, one of the soldiers from Lucas and Travis's company had stalked Kristin, hunting for missing antiquities her brother had stolen. Kristin had been shot in the shoulder, requiring months of physical therapy and counseling before she'd started to feel like her old self again. If anybody knew what Casey was going through right now, it was Kristin. "You've never told me why the two of you broke things off. Every time I ask why it all ended, you change the subject, and Travis has been tight-lipped with Lucas, too."

Because talking about it was humiliating. Painful. Downright depressing. Casey shrugged.

"No. Not this time. This time, you tell me. Because what I really want to know is if I need to walk across the street and punch him in the nose for you."

"Wait." Casey dug her palms into the counter and sat straighter. "Across the street?" Travis was at Lucas's house, which made no sense unless… She held up a hand to stop Kristin's answer. "He's watching me. I ought to be the one to go over there and punch him in the nose."

"He's concerned. I think it's sweet."

"It's not sweet." Casey went to peek between the blinds at Lucas's house, half-surprised not to see Travis sitting on the front porch where Lucas had sat vigil when Kristin was in danger. "It's weird and it's denial. If anybody needs a bodyguard it's him, not me. And if I did need one, it sure wouldn't be him." Still, even as she said the words, the tension in her neck eased. The idea Travis would set aside his life to keep an eye on her was somehow comforting. Just like having him around earlier today. Just like it had been in the past.

Before he'd hurt her.

She dropped her forehead to the window casing. "Travis Heath is a jerk who feels guilty, so he's trying to make up for it since he thinks I'm in danger." Maybe if she told herself that enough, her heart would get the message and let him go.

"I think Travis is a pretty nice guy."

"You never dated him."

"He's funny."

"He thinks he is." Except…he did have a way of making her smile even when she didn't want to.

"He cares about others."

Um, no. Casey drew the line right there. "If he cared so much, he wouldn't have walked out my front door one night like everything was normal and all but disappeared. Ever."

"Wait." From the sound of her voice, Kristin had stood from the couch. "You guys didn't officially break up? He…walked away?"

This was the exact reason Casey had maintained her silence for so long. Kristin was a staunch defender of those she loved, and the last thing Casey needed to do was put her at odds with Travis, who happened to be her fiancé's best friend. Now, though, what did it matter? "Well, he did offer what amounts to a pretty lame explanation for a soldier."

"What explanation?"

Casey lifted one shoulder, keeping her head to the wall. She ran one finger down the sealant around the window casing. It would be awesome if she could seal up her emotions the way the builders had sealed the air out of this house. *Oops, don't want to feel that. We'll just put a little caulk there and nothing can get through.*

Too bad it didn't really work that way. "He decided the army and family don't go together, whatever that means."

"Ouch."

"Exactly. He has a fear of commitment I'm not ever going to be able to overcome. It's better I found out before I fell any harder." Really, Travis had done them both a favor wimping out when he did, and as long as she didn't think too hard about it, his exit didn't bother her at all.

At least, that's what she liked to tell herself.

*But, God? I really don't appreciate Your bringing him now, when there's trouble and he thinks he can play the hero.* Because once this was over, he'd be gone again, like he needed to be.

# EIGHT

The Saturday morning sun streamed through the windows in Lucas's back door, leaving a patchwork of light and shadow on the tile floor. The brightness of the morning did little to lighten Travis's dark mood. Even his third cup of coffee wasn't doing anything more than fueling his need to pace the house.

He'd thought being at Lucas's house, across the street from where Casey was bunking at Kristin's, would make it easier to rest and being within shouting distance would give him peace. He'd been wrong.

He hadn't had many nightmares since he'd left Casey but, boy... Last night had kicked his rear like nothing had since combat.

Wrapping his fingers around the thick brown coffee mug, he let the warmth soak into his palms and through his arms. But it couldn't touch the place inside him that spun in a way he'd never admit to anybody.

Every time he'd tried to sleep, all he'd seen was some crazy blend of present and past, churning like the Gulf of Mexico before a hurricane had leveled their small beach town. John's lifeless eyes shifted and morphed into those of Neil Aiken, the same empty, gone-forever stare marring features alive and laughing a few moments before he stepped on an explosive device.

The device on the path Travis, his team leader, had told him to take point on.

The path Travis should have stepped onto ahead of the men he was leading.

In the end, there was, what, a trade-off? One man for another all because of where they placed their feet? Because Travis had been slack in his own duties and sent one of his soldiers ahead of him, even though his gut was screaming something wasn't right?

Life should be harder to snuff out than it was.

Planting his elbows on the wooden kitchen table, he braced his hands in his short hair and dug his fingers into his scalp, wishing there was a way to dig out the memory once and for all.

Except he wouldn't want to forget.

And he shouldn't have blood on his hands on home soil. He shouldn't be watching his back and hearing footsteps where there were none. He shouldn't have to spend his nights in a cold sweat, terrified Casey was being tortured at the hands of someone he couldn't even see.

"If you fall asleep, try not to drool on my table."

Travis sat back in the chair and forced a grin at Lucas, who came into the kitchen dressed for the run he took with Kristin every weekend morning. "Yeah, well, if you'd invested in a better mattress on the guest-room bed…"

"You'd just better be happy it wasn't a sleeping bag in the backyard, you ungrateful punk." Lucas grinned and grabbed a bottle of water off the counter, took a swig, then swiped at his mouth. "You talk in your sleep. I could hear you through the wall."

"Whatever."

"You have a fantastic attitude this morning, Heath." Lucas slid into the chair across from Travis and thunked his bottle to the table. "You might want to think about dialing it down a little bit."

"Why?"

"I got a call from the first sergeant when Kristin and I were out running."

The way he said it caught Travis's full attention. This was about more than his bad attitude. "Nothing good ever came from that sentence. Wait…" He rolled his eyes to stare at the ceiling, searching his memory, but came up empty. "Nope. Can't think of a single time."

"Nothing good today either."

"Which of your guys got into trouble last night?" As platoon sergeants, the responsibility for their men lay at their feet. Most days, it wasn't a bad deal, but when one of the guys partied too hard, the consequences came swiftly from the chain of command.

"Far as I know, my guys were perfect little soldiers last night. As always." He spun the bottle around then set it onto the table. "This was about you."

Travis's eyebrows drew together, and he tried not to give in to the annoyance pricking at him. There was no reason to go around him. "If the first sergeant needed something from me, he has my number same as yours."

"He wanted to get a read on where your head was before he talked to you. He asked a few questions, I answered, and then I asked him to let me do the talking for him on this one."

The coffee Travis had downed suddenly felt like a really bad idea. "Why am I pretty sure you're about to lay something even worse than I'm imagining on me?"

"There's some concern for your safety after what happened Thursday night and yesterday."

All the air left Travis's lungs in a slow leak. If his chain of command got too worried, there were a lot of moves they could make next, and none of them suited his purposes. "What are you not telling me?"

Lucas rolled his water bottle between his palms, watching the water slosh for a few seconds before he said anything else.

The longer he waited, the more Travis's head pounded.

Finally, Lucas stopped and looked up, pinning Travis with a look he'd used on his soldiers many times. "The commander knew John Winslow, and he knows you." He held up a finger to stop Travis from speaking and kept talking. "They're considering making a serious suggestion you head to post and hunker down at the battalion or somewhere a little less accessible, where it would be harder for—"

"And leave Casey out here alone? No." If anything, he was going to make himself more visible. He was about to let a whole lot of people know Casey wasn't on her own. If they wanted to get to her, they were going to have to come through him. The only way he would hide out on post like some kind of fugitive was if she went with him.

"Do you want to tell me what's going on here?" Lucas said. "You and Casey are practically in hiding already. The first sergeant's worried… You had my back last year when I was watching out for Kristin. No reason you can't give me a chance to do the same."

True. "I don't know. Things don't compute."

"Then start talking and maybe they will."

Travis pressed his spine into the chair, staring at the door. He'd tried to puzzle it out, but the pieces didn't fit. They were almost joined, but there was always one edge that stuck out and ruined the picture. Lucas had a gut instinct Travis had learned to trust over the years, so maybe laying it all out would give his buddy a perspective Travis was too close to see. "At my first duty station, I was part of a Joint Task Force North mission on the border with Mexico."

"The one where you guys tripped over a drug supply line and took out an upstart cartel?"

"See?" Travis dragged his hand across the top of his head. It would be nice if he could smooth out his thoughts as easily as his hair. "It's not like it's some big secret."

"You only bragged about it for half of Ranger School. We all knew."

"You're not funny. Casey's doing a story, and she's interviewed some of the guys who were on the mission with me."

Any amusement on Lucas's face disappeared, and he eased forward to the edge of his chair, elbows on his knees.

Travis had seen the posture about a hundred times. His buddy was sitting on go, ready to do whatever it took to win the coming battle.

"It's not Casey's apartment getting hit or the mugging or even the car. It's Casey's laptop. It was at John's house, and I can't figure out why. She'd already talked to him once and was scheduled to again, so is it something he already said? Something he might say?" Talking about it made the situation more confusing, not less. He ought to stop now, but the worst was yet to come. "Then yesterday, the car on Hay Street. Could have been a second run at her or—"

"Or you're the one somebody's after."

Travis gave a curt nod. If he was the target, then he'd at least know Casey was safe. He'd rather dodge a bullet himself than risk her being hit. There was no doubt losing her would eclipse every other tragedy he'd ever witnessed. "Casey's meeting with Deacon Lewis later today, another guy who was on my team then. I'm going with her whether she wants me to or not. All I can think is I should get Deac's number from Casey and warn him."

"Because if you don't…"

"If I don't, then I might be responsible for his death." Travis dropped his head against the back of the tall wooden chair. "I've had that burden before, and I'm pretty sure I can't live with myself if it happens again."

Casey stared at her sandals, heels dug tightly against the floorboard of Travis's truck.

Once more, they were chasing shadows that might turn out to be figments of their imaginations, or they might turn out to be nightmares.

Travis had pounded on Kristin's door this morning in a foul mood, all traces of his typical humor gone. He'd insisted on calling Deacon this morning, and every call went unanswered. He'd called the police, who didn't see a reason to worry, since Deacon was a grown man who wasn't technically missing. And a call to Marcus had gone to voice mail.

Casey had interviewed Deacon before, for an article on substance abuse in the military, and he'd had his phone on him constantly. He'd laughed once and told her he never went anywhere without it.

Travis had calmed since they were on the move toward Deacon's apartment, but whatever had driven him to make the call still hung in the air and was now seeping deep into her bones. After all they'd been through, anxiety clenched her stomach around the bagel she'd managed to choke down for breakfast. If she made it through this day without growing herself an ulcer, it would shock her.

Travis must have felt her tense. He reached for her but hesitated over the space between them before he dropped his hand next to his leg, thumb working the outer seam of his jeans. "You okay over there?"

No. She wished he'd have closed the gap and touched her hand. Wished she were free to reach over and take his hand herself.

And she hated herself for it.

The heat of anger was safer than the softer emotions trying to swamp her, so Casey gave her all to her frustration. She'd give him one more chance to tell the truth about his attitude this morning before she let her temper take the reins. Being treated like the weak female didn't sit well, even if she was feeling every ounce of weakness down to her bones. "I'd be a whole lot better if you'd give me a clue about what's going on."

The muscles in his cheek tightened, but he merely shook his head. "Nothing. Yesterday would make anybody antsy, even me."

"You're lying." The words leaped out before she could stop them, heating the skin of her cheeks. But the embarrassment dragged out her anger full force. She was in the middle of this, and he didn't get to keep things from her. Before he could do more than drop his jaw to react, she charged on, angling in the seat to face him. "Tell me the truth. Now."

He pulled his attention from the road and looked at her as though she'd sprouted a second nose. He arched an eyebrow in something like wonder, then gripped the steering wheel with both hands, staring out the windshield. "Wow. I didn't know you had so much fire in you, Case."

"Travis…" He didn't get to flatter her into distraction. Not now.

His posture slumped slightly, victory coming a whole lot faster than Casey had anticipated. "My buddy you met yesterday, the cop, Marcus Brewer? He told me to keep an eye on you, and I intend to listen."

Her head drew back, hitting the edge of the headrest. Even though she'd caught Marcus Brewer eyeing her strangely yesterday, she couldn't believe this was the thing that had Travis acting like his fuse was lit and burning fast. "You expect me to believe your buddy thinks I'm in some sort of hot water?"

"Believe me, I wish this was all in my head." He glanced at her again, his fingers kneading the steering wheel as he waited at a stoplight. "This whole mess keeps me thinking… What if you stumbled onto something totally apart from the JTF mission? What if there's something bigger going on? I know it looks like I'm the target, but nobody's broken into my house and stolen my stuff. And now Deacon's missing. Nothing makes sense."

"Deacon's not missing. He's just not answering his phone. Maybe he left it on the kitchen counter. Maybe he's on a breakfast date. Or in the shower and we're going to look like idiots pounding on his door." Even knowing Deacon as little as she did, Casey knew every one of those reasons was lame. Still, once in this whole mess, she'd like for the easy thing to be true.

Watching another car drive through the intersection, Travis said, "Don't ignore the fact we were nearly run down yesterday." His voice held an edge Casey had rarely heard, not anger but something slightly more jagged.

They weren't having this argument again. Casey sighed and stared out the front window as Travis hung a left into Deacon's apartment complex. They were both trying to make coherent sentences out of alphabet soup, when everything refused to come together. "I'm not ready to believe somebody's after me. You're the more plausible target." Sure, she said the words out loud, but Casey wasn't ready to admit she hadn't slept well last night, knowing someone had been in her apartment, had violated her space. The theft of her computers didn't fit neatly into her whole "they're only after Travis" theory. She'd distinctly heard every creak Kristin's old house made, certain footsteps crept up the hallway. But, yeah, she'd keep it to herself.

Travis backed into a space next to a dark gray sedan and shoved the truck into Park before turning to her, the leather seat creaking. He started counting on his fingers as he spoke. "First, you and I are mugged in the parking lot at a Mexican restaurant. Second, John's killed and your laptop is at the scene. Third, we're targeted in the middle of Hay Street. Fourth, your apartment is hit. Now Deacon's gone off the grid?" His gaze pinned on hers, his mouth a grim line. "I'm out of fingers to count on, and I don't buy such a long string of coincidences."

Apparently, they were having this argument again after all. "Then you're the one who should be worried, because the target isn't me. It's you." She ticked off a list of her own. "The mugging, John's murder, the hit-and-run, Deacon… You're a stronger connection than I am."

For the smallest second, her assertion hit home. Doubt flickered across his features, but then he raised one shoulder in a dismissive shrug. "You said revenge yesterday, but I don't buy it. Not this many years later." He held up a hand, stopping her next argument. "Your laptop. Your computers at your apartment. To me, those are compelling bits of evidence. Casey, this is about you."

"Unless they think I have information on…" The words died. All she could see was her familiar computer case, spattered with John's blood. Her chin dropped and she studied her hands twisted together in her lap. "I don't know." The words barely qualified as a whisper, hardly audible in the silence of the truck.

"Casey, listen…" Travis leaned closer, the warmth of him palpable in the air-conditioned cab of the pickup. "I want you to think about packing up and staying somewhere on post for a while. I don't want to scare you, but—" The words stopped and his breath quickened.

Lifting her head, Casey expected to see him staring at her, but he was focused on something out the windshield.

"Travis?"

He didn't answer her. Instead, Travis leaned forward slightly, watching something at the front of the apartment building. The lines around his mouth tightened as his brow furrowed.

Casey turned to look over her shoulder. "What do you—" Her heart slammed against her ribs, and she instinctively unclasped her seat belt as Travis whipped around in the seat and shoved his door open, out of the truck before Casey could finish her question.

She reached for the door handle to follow him but stopped and bit back a scream. In the gray sedan beside them, Deacon Lewis slumped over the steering wheel.

# NINE

Travis slid down in the vinyl chair in the emergency waiting room and stretched his legs, dragging his palms down his cheeks. If things didn't ease soon, he was going to have to head to Kristin's basement gym and go a few rounds with a punching bag. Either that or his body was going to turn itself inside out from the tension.

The waiting area of the emergency room hummed with noise and smelled like hospitals always seemed to smell, the antiseptic odor nobody would ever claim to like. It sure wasn't sitting well with him.

He'd ignored his gut last night. Because he hadn't called Deacon sooner, his former friend was somewhere in this hospital, possibly fighting for his life.

Once again, he'd failed.

Beside him, Casey shifted, her knee brushing his thigh. It was the first contact she'd made since they'd found Deacon unconscious in his car, and it jolted into his chest, same as it had when they'd first started dating and he'd felt like the biggest man in the world because he got to hold her hand.

Those months felt like decades ago. He'd left and,

right now, he couldn't remember why. With the world spinning around him, all he wanted was to rewind to three months ago and undo the damage. Maybe then she'd be safe. Maybe then he'd have the right to draw her to him and shield her from whatever came next.

Maybe then he wouldn't be staring at a report date to selection for a unit that would ask everything of him.

Casey sighed and turned her knees away, leaving the spot she'd brushed somehow colder than the rest of him. "At least Deacon was alive when we found him." Her voice was thin, almost lost in the conversation buzzing in the room.

Small consolation. Deacon had a gray look about him, his pulse thready, his breathing shallow. Another few minutes and they might have been too late. The thought rocked Travis, images from the past three days swirling together. Too late for John and too many near misses for them. He ran his thumb along the road rash in his palm, where he'd landed hard on Hay Street as the car sped past, the sting dragging him into the moment.

Too much was happening, and he didn't know how to make it stop.

Without letting himself second-guess the consequences, he reached for Casey's hand and laced his fingers through hers, searching for something to hold, seeking something to remind him they were still alive.

Desperate to protect her. The clues pointed everywhere, and figuring out who was in danger was growing more impossible every second.

Casey hesitated, her fingers stiff, but then, like ice cream melting on a July day, they softened and curled around his to send a warmth up his arm and into the deepest part of him.

He hadn't realized how cold he was.

It must have shown because she held on tighter. "What are you thinking that's got your face looking like you downed one too many of Kristin's oranges?"

Travis allowed himself a slight smile. Man, she'd been able to read him since the day she met him. Rarely did she say anything out loud, but she'd always followed his thoughts wherever they rambled. Looked like some things never changed. "I'm thinking I'm an idiot." He slid his feet closer to his chair to let a woman and her small son pass, then stretched out again.

"You saved Deacon's life. If you hadn't thought so fast and decided we needed to go to his apartment instead of waiting…" Casey shuddered, her fingers tightening around his. "We made it in time. Deacon has made it this far. Hopefully, he'll make it all the way. I keep praying. So, no. You're far from an idiot."

Maybe he wasn't an idiot where Deacon was concerned, but he sure had been with Casey. More than anything, he wanted to tell her, then to call the chain of command and tell them he was needed here more than he was needed at selection.

But his thought shouldn't be there. He shoved aside the past and said another quick prayer Deacon would survive whatever had happened to him. Travis hadn't stopped praying since the moment he'd spotted Deacon slumped over his steering wheel, heavy and limp. "We should have at least let him know sooner John was dead. It might have put his guard up."

"Those kinds of things are easy to think now. You can't beat yourself to pieces for not knowing the future.

Realistically, you couldn't have seen this coming. Right now, you can only do what you're having Lucas do—call the rest of your men to tell them this is happening."

Clamping his teeth on the tip of his tongue, Travis pulled his hand from Casey's and sat forward, elbows on his knees, staring at the tile floor. Those words were almost exactly what his commander had said after Neil Aiken died. *Nobody could have seen it coming.*

Well, Travis should have. He was supposed to be vigilant at all times, was supposed to anticipate the next attack. Overseas, he'd missed it, wrapped in his own exhaustion and his own needs when the threat had been right beneath their feet. This time, he'd been so caught up in protecting Casey and trying to put the pieces together, he'd missed the bigger picture. His former teammates were in danger, just as she'd argued. Whether it was because of something Casey was doing or because of the op all those years ago didn't matter. Whether Casey was also a target or not didn't change anything. They were in danger. And he'd missed it because he was focused on her.

As much as he would give to touch Casey again, he wouldn't. He couldn't. He needed to take a step away, to think about this logically, the way he'd been trained, without the scent of vanilla and apples that always hovered around her.

If he walked away for a minute to clear his head, she'd be safe. An armed security guard stood by the door, watching the room. The waiting area was packed, and Travis was certain no one would approach her in such a closed environment.

Shoving his hands against his knees, he stood and stared across the room, not even daring to look at her.

If he caught her eye, he'd waver. "I need a cup of coffee and some fresh air. I'm going to walk around the outside to the main lobby. You want to hang here in case they come out with news about Deacon?"

She started to stand, then sank in her chair with the weight of his implied *leave me alone*. Without looking, he knew her shoulders would be slouched the way they did when she felt she was being left behind. Travis wished he could explain. He wasn't leaving her.

Except he was.

He was running away. Again. He couldn't tell her why because he didn't know the reason himself. All he knew was he had to get away.

"I'll stay. I'll text you if anything happens." Her voice was heavy, the weight dragging him to her.

Giving in would be so easy, but if he did, he'd wrap her in his arms and never let go. That wouldn't be good for either of them. He'd hurt her, get close for a few days then back away when he had to leave, cutting them both.

Exiting the doors near the parking lot, Travis inhaled the humid afternoon heat, grateful to be free of the stifling weight of the air inside. Skirting cars and taking the long way around the parking deck, he entered the main lobby. He was halfway to the coffee cart when the sound of his name stopped him.

Phil Ingram crossed the lobby from a far hallway in long strides, concern etching his features. "Travis." He stopped and clamped a hand on Travis's shoulder. "What are you doing here?"

"Phil." Travis eased himself from Phil's grasp. When he'd broken things off with Casey, the hurt had nearly thrown him backward into the worst version of himself, especially when he stopped by Phil's and the man offered him a beer to take the edge off, one of the very habits Travis had fought to kick.

Some friend.

Right now, he definitely didn't need any more voices added to the noise in his head. This conversation had to end quickly. "Buddy of mine had to go to the ER." With the investigation ongoing, he wasn't sure what he could say, and there wasn't much he wanted to say to Phil anyway.

"Scared me, seeing you here." Phil looked relieved. "Hey, I just wrapped a class on nutrition for pregnant mothers. You need anything while you wait? Want to grab a bite in the cafeteria? They have a mean chicken sandwich. Been a while since we talked."

Travis forced a smile. Why he'd vanished was not a discussion he wanted to have right now…or ever. "Things got a little crazy."

"From what I saw on the news, it's getting crazier."

"What are you saying?" He hadn't bothered with the news in days. If something in the world was about to have them wheels up and shipped out to parts unknown before he knew Casey was safe, he wasn't sure how he'd make it through.

"We saw the news story about John Winslow. You were in one of the wide shots. You were there?"

The knots inside him unwound. Only his immediate world was out of control. "I went with Casey to interview him for a story."

Phil nodded, his expression grim. "Sounds like it was pretty bad." He glanced at his watch, then in the direction of the cafeteria. "John and I hung around together some after you deployed. Do you know if Casey got what she needed before he died?"

The spin in this conversation almost made Travis dizzy. It was as though Phil couldn't focus on one thing longer than ten seconds. "I couldn't—" His phone vibrated in his pocket, and he pulled it out to glance at the screen.

Deacon's in a room. Asking for me.

Travis's muscles tensed for action. "I have to go." He threw a confused Phil an abrupt wave and jogged for the hall to the ER, mind racing.

If Deacon was asking for Casey, then maybe the answers they needed were about to fall right into their hands.

She shouldn't have texted him.

Travis's great escape from the waiting room had everything to do with her. It was obvious. The way he'd tensed when she touched him had told the whole story. He was even less interested now than he had been months ago.

Yet somehow he kept showing up where she was.

And she needed him.

Whether Travis needed her or not, she needed him, more now than ever. Things kept getting weirder, and the more she tried to put it all together, the more her brain felt like scrambled eggs.

It was becoming painfully obvious she couldn't get through this without somebody beside her, no matter how much she wanted to. And no matter how much she didn't want the person who had let her fall in the past be the one she leaned on in the present.

"Case."

She jumped. He'd come in behind her through the hospital, not the way he'd left.

And again with the nickname. All her life, she'd hated when somebody shortened her given name, but Travis had called her Case from day one. She ought to tell him to stop.

But it felt too good to hear it.

She closed her eyes and took a second to prepare for the sight of him, then turned.

He looked like he'd run a marathon. His eyes were wider than usual, bright with something that looked like anger or fear. His face was flushed as though he'd sprinted the length of the hallway.

Probably because he wanted to hear what Deacon had to say.

"How's Deac? Did they tell you?"

Yep. Information on Deacon's condition was all he wanted. Casey swallowed her disappointment. "All I know is they put him in a regular room and he's asking for…" It sounded strange to say it out loud.

"You."

She nodded once. "I have no idea why. It's not like…" She shrugged. "He should have asked for you. You're the one who saved his life."

"But he's smart. He knows the better half of this duo is you." Travis grabbed her hand, wrapping his fingers around hers and tugging her gently toward the door leading to the main hall. "Let's go. Looks like he's got something he wants to say to you."

Rather than get dragged along like a reluctant child,

Casey kept pace. Travis would let go at any second, once she caught up.

But he didn't. He held tight all the way through the halls, in the elevator and to the door of Deacon Lewis's private room.

Travis stopped and glanced at Casey and squeezed her hand. "You ready?"

No. But she couldn't quit now, not when the man who might have answers lay a few feet away. Casey nodded.

Travis pushed the door open and dropped her hand to usher her in with his palm against the small of her back.

The warmth of his touch, the way it ran along her spine and supported her in spite of everything, the familiarity of the gesture—something he'd done every time they'd walked through a doorway when they were dating—made Casey want to stop and lean against him. To pretend, if only for a moment, this wasn't a hospital and neither one of them was in danger.

Instead, she stiffened her spine and outpaced him into the room. Although it was late afternoon, the space was dark after the bright lights of the hallway. In the stillness, the low hum of machines overwhelmed the room.

Deacon lay propped in the bed, his eyes closed, an oxygen mask obscuring the lower half of his face. His dark skin was almost gray against the white sheets.

At the window, a woman turned toward them, her dark hair cut in a pixie that waved against her scalp, a barely concealed anger distorting her features before she reset to a neutral expression. "I thought you were the doctor again." She walked toward them but didn't extend her hand. "Gwen Mitchell."

Travis stepped aside and let Casey take the lead. The gesture took her memory to others like it, times when he'd stood aside and let her have the spotlight. How had she not noticed before?

Gwen's eyebrow arched, and Casey realized she hadn't responded. "I'm sorry. I'm Casey Jordan. This is Travis Heath."

Gwen gave a brief nod, but her expression didn't warm. "Deac's barely been awake, but the first person he asked for was you, Ms. Jordan. How do you know my fiancé?"

Beside her, Travis took a quick breath, and Casey understood the other woman's coldness. Her lips parted slightly, a wave of guilt washing over her, although she'd done nothing wrong. "No. It's…" Her jaw worked for a moment and she winced, then tried again. "I interviewed Deacon for an article a few months ago. He's the one who gave me the idea for the story I'm working on now." She fished in her small purse for a business card and passed one to Gwen. "I work for Public Affairs on post, and I was supposed to meet Deacon today to interview him. There's no… I mean, there's nothing to…worry about." There was wasn't a way to finish an explanation like that gracefully, but it was a little embarrassing being thought of as the kind of woman who'd bust up a relationship.

Gwen glanced at Travis, then at the card, her expression remaining neutral. "For the cartel story. He told me but didn't tell me who he was talking to." She pocketed the business card and let her eyes rest on Deacon, who hadn't moved. "It's not easy when your man's in the hospital and then he looks at you and asks for another woman."

"I bet not." Travis's voice came over her shoulder, heavy with sympathy.

Gwen's mouth quirked then, and her face softened. She laid a hand on Deacon's wrist. "He went to sleep, but he should wake up any minute. He's been in and out since they brought him in."

Travis eased closer to Casey. "What did the doctors say?"

Shaking her head, Gwen backed away from the bed as tears glistened in the corners of her eyes. "They're still running tests, but the first round…" The lines around her mouth deepened. "He overdosed on a depressant. Nearly stopped his heart."

Casey gasped and reached for the bed rail, trying to steady herself. That couldn't be true. If she'd known Gwen better, she'd have hugged the woman and tried to comfort her. If the news about Deacon was this shocking to her, it had to be even worse for the woman who loved him. "When I talked to Deacon for the last story, he said he'd been clean for years. And he never mentioned depressants. He was in recovery for using…" She might have said too much. There was no way of knowing how much Gwen knew about her fiancé's past.

Face grim, Gwen nodded. "He was abusing prescription meds for ADHD, looking for a high, not a low. He'd been in recovery several months when I met him. There hasn't been any sign he's using, so it's hard for me to believe he'd…" She inhaled deeply and lifted her head. "Thing is, the doctors think this overdose was by injection and—" she gestured to his arm "—no tracks."

Travis stiffened. "What do the police say?"

"Not much yet. To them, he's an addict who took it too far."

"No." The voice from the bed was weak, but the tone was sure.

Gwen turned toward Deacon and leaned over him, pasting a smile on her face, the lines around her mouth belying the tension she tried to hide. "You been listening this whole time?"

Deacon squeezed his eyes shut, then opened them again, lasering in on Casey, then sliding to Travis, widening when he spotted his former teammate. He slid the mask down his face slowly, like the movement was painful. "Heath?"

Easy grin firmly in place, Travis slipped around the bed to stand closer to his old friend. "Believe it or not."

When he spoke, the tension in the room eased. Casey envied his calm demeanor, the relaxed way he handled the situation, as though he saved people from near-death experiences every day.

Which, come to think of it, he might actually do sometimes.

"Am I dead or something?" Deacon's voice was barely above a whisper, but the words grew stronger.

"No." Gwen smoothed Deacon's close-cropped dark hair. "You're alive thanks to these two."

Deacon's face darkened as he looked at Casey.

Travis slipped an arm around her waist. Somehow, he knew she was going to waver if he didn't support her. Yet another thing she'd missed about him.

"Sorry, Casey." Deacon took a labored breath. "I didn't answer any calls. Didn't want to meet with you. Shouldn't have agreed to." His voice grew softer, and he slid the oxygen mask into place, closing his eyes and inhaling deeply.

Casey leaned closer, wanting to shake him, to beg him to explain why he'd asked for her, why he hadn't wanted to meet with her, to see if he had answers to who was after Travis…or her. Instead, she stared at the man lying helpless before her. *Don't fall asleep. Please.*

"Maybe we should wait until later." Gwen shifted toward the door, but Deacon's eyes opened again.

He pulled the mask away and kept his attention on Casey. "No. You should know."

Travis's fingers tightened on Casey's as her heart marched double time. Whatever Deacon had to say, it was likely going to turn their world on its head again.

There wasn't much more she could take. Her feet ached to run, but before she could tug Travis to the door and bolt the way she wanted to, Deacon lowered the mask again. "Heard Winslow died. Didn't want to face you. Didn't want you to figure out I was using again." He glanced at Gwen, then at Travis and to Casey, his expression dark with regret. "John was my supplier."

# TEN

Leaning against the wall outside Deacon's room, Travis rested his head and stared at the ceiling. Over the course of the past twenty-four hours, as whatever he had overdosed on worked its way out of his system, Deacon had grown stronger, though he couldn't tell them anything about a large chunk of the previous morning. He wouldn't say what he'd used, probably well aware the police were going to have questions.

Travis had spent another restless night at Lucas's before accompanying Casey to her church, raising more than a few questioning stares neither of them had felt like explaining. When it became clear they were both destined to pace Kristin's house for the rest of the afternoon, Casey had suggested they visit Deacon once again to learn if he had more to share.

With his head on straighter than it had been the night before, Deacon had grown more tight-lipped about John, acting as though he hadn't said anything about their former teammate, instead deflecting Casey's questions.

Well, Travis had questions, too. As soon as the doctor who'd gone in to check on Deacon was done, those questions were going to get a response. If John had been dealing, there was a good possibility the answers to his death lay in a hospital room with the sole link they had to him.

In a small waiting area at the end of the hall, Casey paced in front of a large window. She'd been silent ever since Deacon had shut her out, and Travis hadn't pushed her to talk. He knew from past history that she'd spill what was on her mind once she'd worked it through.

While she was occupied with her thoughts and with whatever lay outside the window, Travis took his time studying her, the first chance he'd really gotten to do so since he'd seen her in the Mexican restaurant, talking to John and sparking jealousy he hadn't been prepared to face.

She was still the most beautiful woman he'd ever spoken to. Even now, her blond hair twisted into a hasty ponytail as they'd rushed out of Kristin's house, dressed in jeans and a T-shirt from some little town in the mountains. There wasn't another woman who could capture his attention the way she did. Sure, over the years he'd done his fair share of hopping from relationship to relationship, but he'd given up those ways, given his life to Jesus, and settled down before Casey came into his life. And when she had, she'd caught his heart like no other woman ever had.

The timing of her entrance into his life made no sense. For years, he'd been certain God had called him to pay for his mistakes by being the kind of soldier Neil Aiken would have been.

Knowing what he needed to do hadn't stopped him from falling for Casey the first time, though. With her, he hadn't needed to chase after anything else to be happy. The greatest moments of their time together had come when she'd looked exactly like she did right now. They hadn't needed to go bar hopping or dancing or whatever to have fun. All he'd needed was a good movie on TV, take-out boxes scattered all over the coffee table, and her head on his shoulder. Chasing adrenaline and soldiering on hadn't been nearly so satisfying.

But when fear slammed him sideways, God brought Travis's mission into focus. He'd considered telling Casey everything, but having never discussed what he believed God was telling him to do, having never confessed his part in Aiken's death or his rowdy drinking days, it had been too hard. After he'd left her apartment, he'd paced his bedroom in the darkness, wrestling with fear and his feelings for the woman he wanted to spend the rest of his life with.

Ultimately, as the sky tinged with light, he'd come to the decision he'd always known what to do and Casey had distracted him. Like a coward, he'd run.

He'd felt like half of himself ever since.

Now, selection loomed ever closer, and he had no idea how he was going to walk away from her again, especially with a threat looming over her safety. He only knew every time he thought of losing her, his blood seemed to slow in his veins, and the same cold panic rushed along his spine.

When he was in high school, reckless and always seeking the next big adrenaline rush, he'd gotten the bright idea to follow the lead of some buddies who were going to surf the Gulf in the roughed-up waters of an offshore hurricane. It was something he'd seen guys do while he was growing up in Pensacola, but he'd never had the guts to try. He'd held his own for quite a while, then been tumbled by a rogue wave and driven into shore, flipped over and over as the water churned around him, unsure which way was up or if he'd ever breathe air again.

The same sensation swamped him now, a panicked drowning, but he couldn't figure out why. Because bad guys lurked around every corner? Or because Casey Jordan might be their target?

He had to keep her safe, or die trying.

Something in the air changed. Travis blinked hard against the hallway lights and realized Casey was staring at him, an unspoken question hanging between them.

Probably because he was staring at her.

What he ought to do was march over there and explain everything, from the moment he'd watched Neil Aiken die until today. Maybe talking to her would help wipe away the fear. Maybe it would sort out the wants and the needs and the had-tos.

He straightened to go to her, but the door to Deacon's room opened and Gwen came out with the doctor right behind her.

The doctor aimed a finger at the nurse's station. "They should be able to answer your question." With a brief glance at Travis, he led Gwen up the hallway.

Deacon was alone. Which meant Travis might get some answers.

Casey met him at the door. "Did they say how he is?"

"No. But I want a minute with him by myself."

Her eyes narrowed. "Why?"

"We worked together. Went into combat together.

There are a couple of things I want to ask him and a couple of answers we need, and he might be a little more willing to talk to me than to you."

Her head jerked like he'd insulted her. "But I'm the one who—" Her teeth dug into her lower lip and she nodded, though she refused to meet his eyes. "Know what? You're right." Without the argument he'd expected, she turned and strode to the waiting area to resume her vigil at the window.

Travis wanted to go to her and explain he wasn't trying to shut her out, but both of them knew he was right. Anything else he said would sound as though he was patronizing her.

With a quick knock, he slipped into Deacon's room, hoping the other man wasn't asleep again.

Thankfully, he was sitting in the bed, staring at the door, no longer in need of the oxygen mask that had hindered him the day before. A shadow crossed his face when Travis entered, then cleared into something that might have been resignation. "Bet you have questions."

Shutting the door behind him, Travis crossed the room and stood over his former squad mate. Back in the day, they'd gone through quite a lot together, and he'd never seen any indication Deacon would seek out anything to dull the pain. Unlike Travis, who'd already been drinking too hard, trying to forget previous deployments when the one he shared with John and Deacon came around. "I guess I'm wondering what happened."

"The guy who went swimming in a bottle every chance he got has to ask?" The question wasn't harsh, simply matter-of-fact.

Still, it caught Travis on the blind side. It took a

second for him to regain his voice. "Fine. You're right. But you and John both?"

Deacon turned his head and stared at the window, where daylight had dimmed into late evening. "Some people are bad for you from the get-go. John was one, and both of us should never have gotten in with…" He sucked his tongue against his teeth and shook his head.

Oh no. Deacon didn't get to stop there, not when it seemed like an answer might be on the tip of his tongue. "Gotten involved with who?"

There was no response. Just the hard shell of an expression saying Deacon was finished talking.

It was clear he wasn't going to say anything else, even if Travis had all night to wait, which he didn't. Gwen could return at any second. He changed direction. "I was with John when he died."

Deacon stiffened but didn't indicate he'd heard otherwise.

Digging his heels into the floor, Travis fired the question he most wanted the answer to. "He was pretty desperate to get out his last word. He said 'bet,' Deac. That mean anything to you?"

If it was possible, Deacon's skin paled even more. He looked at Travis, his expression deathly serious. "Listen to me good, Heath. Forget you heard anything."

"But—"

"I mean it. Don't go looking for trouble."

The warning crawled across Travis's neck. "I'm not sure I understand what you're saying."

"I'm pretty sure you've already had one warning. Listen to it. You have a good life going for you, and if what I see is any indication, a good woman. Unless you want to lose both, you'll get you and her as far from this building as possible and then you'll stay out of this. For good."

Casey dropped to the couch in the small waiting area tucked into an alcove at the end of the hallway and dragged her hand along the vinyl. The last time she'd been this bone weary had been during deployment, and it was a feeling she hated to her very core. How she'd landed here, in the middle of a hurricane of confusion and misunderstanding, was beyond her. All she knew was the storm blew in with Travis Heath and didn't show any signs of blowing out anytime soon.

She settled into the vinyl sofa and closed her eyes, trying to drown out the low voices and quiet footfalls in the hallways around her. The past few days were catching up to her, and now, with night falling yet again, helplessness crept in to overtake the edges of fear.

As much as she hated to admit it, Travis had a better chance of getting Deacon to talk than she did. Still, it stung a little. This was her story. Deacon was her source. While Travis had been perfectly polite and entirely right, the whole thing made Casey feel as though she was losing control. Coupled with the fear dogging her and the lack of sleep that had marked her nights, she was finished. If she could, she'd run away to the deep woods where nobody could take aim at her ever again.

"Casey, right?" The deep male voice fell from above.

Jumping at the sound, Casey scrambled up and tried to get her bearings, muscles tensed in preparation for a fight.

A vaguely familiar man held out his hands, palms first, a smile tipping the corner of his mouth. "Sorry.

Didn't mean to scare you. Thought I recognized you and wanted to see if you needed anything."

Mind spinning, Casey sorted through her memories, trying to catch the one that held this man's face. As he lowered his hands, bandaged across the knuckles, the image clicked. She snapped her fingers. "I'm sorry. The coffee shop. You're... Phillip?"

"Close enough. I prefer Phil." He gestured to the couch and waited for her to sit before he settled into a chair at a right angle from her. "I ran into Travis in the lobby yesterday. He said he was visiting a friend. I hope you're not the one he was talking about, are you?"

Casey willed her mind to stop racing. The guy had made Travis antsy at the coffee shop on Friday, but he seemed friendly enough, with a smile that reached his dark eyes and an easy way of speaking, as though he'd known her forever. "No. A mutual friend. Travis is with him now." She relaxed enough to offer him a smile in return. "I see you got somebody to doctor your hands."

"What?" Confusion skated across his face, then he glanced at his fingers, which rested on his knees. "Oh. Yeah. Meredith insisted. I thought it made me look tough. She thought it looked like a recipe for infection." He leaned closer as though he was going to share some deep secret. "I can tell you from working here and from being married to her... Whether they take care of people or pets, all doctors are the same."

Casey grinned. "You're a doctor, as well?"

"No way. I can't handle blood. I spend my time in a classroom teaching people about nutrition or addiction or whatever else they ask me to teach to the staff or the community. It's a lot quieter and a lot less messy." He glanced at his watch, then scanned the hallway. "So, when we met on Friday, you said you work for Public Affairs?"

"I do." As inane as the conversation was, it was exactly what Casey needed. "Like any other job, it has good days and bad, but I'm pretty sure I wouldn't trade it."

"Sounds like you're pretty happy then." Phil propped his ankle on his knee and watched the nurses at their station. The silence was comfortable, if a little long, before he spoke again. "You said you were going back to a previous story?"

Talking to strangers about her work had always been hard. Until a story was finished, it always felt like there was some vague chance it wouldn't work out the way she wanted, so she kept it close to the vest. "Working on a follow-up to some things from a few months ago, looking at a drug story from a different angle. The usual."

"Hmm." A shadow flickered across his face. He settled both feet flat on the floor and scooted forward in the chair as though he were about to stand. "It's been a long couple of days around here, and I'm guessing it's been even longer for you if the way you were half-asleep when I walked up is any indication. Got a coffeemaker in my office if you want something a little stronger than the cafeteria serves. And if you're looking for a place to crash for a little while, there's a couch and a blanket. I'm headed out so all you'd need to do is lock the door when you leave. It's a lot quieter there than it is here."

Casey flicked a glance toward Deacon's room. As worn out as she felt, the offer was tempting, but Travis would worry if he came out and she was nowhere to be found.

Following her gaze, Phil leaned closer. "I'll tell the nurses to let Travis know where you are, if you're afraid he'll be worried."

Enticed by the idea of a few moments of actual alone time, Casey started to agree, but Travis came out of Deacon's room and caught her eye. Even from a distance, she could read the question on his face when he caught sight of Phil.

He was beside her so fast Casey almost didn't have time to blink. His arm slipped around her waist in a way that said *back off.* "Phil. Working late?"

Casey wanted to pull away from him, but the warmth of his arm around her was exactly what she'd been longing for. She felt safer than she had in days, confident Travis would never let anything happen to her.

Later, when he wasn't touching her, she could lecture him about the fact he had no right to act like a jealous boyfriend. For now, she sank against him and let herself pretend he really did have the right to warn another man away from her, not caring how bad it would hurt when he eventually walked away again.

Phil glanced toward the elevator. "I saw Casey sitting there, so I thought I'd see if she needed anything."

"We're leaving." Travis's arm around Casey tightened. "See you." With a pressure at her waist, he urged Casey past Phil and up the hall to the elevator.

The doors had closed behind them before he dropped his arm, leaving Casey to abandon her illusions.

It cut, exactly the way she'd known it would. The

pain left her angry at both of them. "What was that all about?"

Sinking against the wall, Travis shoved his hands in his pockets, looking as though he'd expected her outburst all along. "I know. It was rude. It was territorial. Got it."

"If you've 'got it,' then why did you do it?"

He lifted his head, the glint in his eye hard, warning her she better not argue. "Because I've got to get you somewhere out of the way. The sooner, the better."

# ELEVEN

"Unless Deacon said something bordering on insane, I think you're overreacting."

When Travis didn't answer, Casey clamped down on her lower lip. She'd been asking for half an hour, and he'd been silent.

Twisting the key in the lock of the old farmhouse, Casey shoved her shoulder against wood swollen with late-summer humidity. The door burst into the kitchen, practically dumping her in a sprawl across the cracked linoleum flooring. The sweet, musty smell of a house closed for too long greeted her, the air hot and heavy. With practiced aim, she found the light switch with one swipe, illuminating the old kitchen.

It looked the same as it had a month ago, when she'd driven out to check on the property for her parents. The same as it had when her great-grandfather passed away six years earlier. Antique kitchen utensils hung from the white walls. The ancient harvest gold appliances sat in place, while the familiar metal-and-Formica kitchen table held court in the middle of the room. The sagging leather couch where she'd taken many an afternoon nap covered by a brown-and-orange crocheted afghan waited against the wall under the window. This was home, pure and simple. Sure, it could use some TLC, but every time she walked through the door, she expected to see Greepaw limping in from the den, arms wide for a hug.

Behind her, Travis shut the door, leaned against the wood and gave a low whistle. "It looks like it did the last time we were out here."

He could have said anything else. Casey did her best not to look at him as she crossed the kitchen. If his expression indicated regret, it would be so much worse than if he showed no emotion at all. In the small, dark-paneled den, Casey let her feet sink into the shag carpeting and slid the thermostat lower. Thankfully, Greepaw had given in back in the '80s and let her parents install central heat and air.

Air-conditioning sure couldn't do anything to make Travis's comment more comfortable. The last time they'd been out here, talk had run to the future. They'd sat on the green chenille couch in the den and talked until dawn about what they'd do to improve the place if she bought it from her parents. He'd caught her vision of replica 1950s' appliances in the kitchen and white vinyl siding over the faded exterior.

She'd been into the house twice since then, both times at her parents' request. When she came to Gray's Creek now, it was to the woods clearing where her great-grandfather had taught her how to raise a bow and sight down the arrow to hit the target. But to the house? No. The place bore Travis's mark. She'd absorbed his thoughts about the house and made them hers, could see him here with her. Those thoughts hazed over happier memories from her childhood.

When she came into the kitchen, Travis hadn't left the doorway. Somewhere in his mind, he was bound to be remembering the times he'd visited the house with her. If he wasn't, he was heartless.

She dropped to the creaking couch and stared at the table, not quite ready to look him in the eye. "Travis, why are we here? Wasn't Kristin's house enough so-called safety? What did Deacon say to make you speak rudely to a friend then drag me out here in the middle of the night?"

"Believe me, Phil's no friend." His voice was bitter as he shoved away from the door and dropped the bag holding the remains of their drive-through dinner on the table.

Casey hazarded a glance at his face. His blue eyes were tired, deep lines etching around them. He looked more haggard than she'd ever seen him. It was more than weariness. There was a pain there that had haunted him since he'd blown into her life.

Her blood felt as though it slowed in her veins. Something was wrong, and it was more than what had happened behind a closed hospital door. "Talk to me."

He stared at the bold flowered curtains covering the window above her. "Deacon told me to stop digging and I should get you somewhere safe."

Not what she'd expected to hear. At all. "He knows more than he's saying."

"A lot more."

Frustration gnawed at her. Frustration with Deacon for holding out on them, with herself for being out of control, and with Travis for…everything. "Well, great, but we can't stay out here indefinitely. We have work tomorrow. For the army. They aren't going to take 'my ex thinks I'm in danger' as an excuse for my not show-ing up. You already took Friday afternoon off at the last minute, and your chain of command will ask ques-tions if you pull a stunt like that again. It's not like we can call in sick, you know."

"I know." He snapped off the words, then winced. "Sorry." Dragging his hands down his face, he dropped to the couch beside her. "Give me this much. Tonight, we stay out here. I've got a uniform in the truck, and I'll take you home in the morning and follow you to work."

"You're going to tail me everywhere?"

"If I have to."

The no-nonsense tone sent the best kind of shivers along her arms, the same kind she'd felt the last time they were out here. Four words, but they spoke of more. Protection. Safety. Comfort.

She swallowed the lump in her throat. He hadn't meant it the way it sounded. She was overly tired and emotional, and he was still the same Travis, focused on the job. Soon, he'd be gone to a unit that would take him away anywhere in the world at any time he was needed. She wouldn't ask him to give up his dream. But for tonight, she'd stop fighting his need to play protec-tor. Having him near dulled the edges of her fear and helped her to feel less vulnerable.

Easing into the corner, she tucked her feet under-neath her and rested her head on the back of the couch, searching for a neutral subject. "You ought to know nothing's going to change here. This house will look the same until Mom decides she can let it go. The house has been in the family for generations. She's having a hard time."

"So you haven't admitted you want to buy it from

her." The comment was intimate, the reminder of conversations past, of how well they'd once known each other.

"No." Casey poked her pinkie through a hole in the afghan and stared at her fingernail. She'd wanted the house since Greepaw died, long before she'd met Travis. But he'd visited the house with her on so many occasions... Now she could hardly stand to walk through the door.

Sitting with him, in the silence broken by the low hum of the air conditioner, was already tying her stomach in knots with a potent blend of longing and fear. She was too tired to fight. She nestled deeper into the couch and stifled a yawn. "Tell me about Phil."

"Not much to tell."

"Liar." She said the word gently, taking away some of the sting.

His mouth quirked, but he kept his focus on the sink across the kitchen. "He was a friend. Once. Kind of guy who had a good ear when you had a problem."

"What happened?"

"I went to him for help one night, and he offered me a beer to take the edge off."

Wrinkling her eyebrows, Casey lifted her head. He'd likely meant it to be an offhand comment, but his tone held a weight running counter to the simplicity of his words. "You don't drink." At least not that she'd ever seen. "There's a reason, isn't there?"

He nodded once and shifted, running his hands down his legs and digging his fingers into his thighs the way he always did when wrestling with something inside. She'd seen the quirk more than once when they were dating and even more over the past few days as the pressure increased.

This time, though, there was a sadness saying this was more than what they were enduring together. Her heart went to him, wondering what could have worked its way into his soul so deeply.

Without caring what her actions might hint, only knowing he needed someone to be alongside him, she shifted in her seat and laid her head on his shoulder, sliding her hand down his arm to lace her fingers through his. Deep inside, she had to admit it wasn't only for him. She needed him, too.

Travis stiffened as though he were going to pull away, but then his fingers curled around hers and he relaxed, sitting for a long time before he spoke again. "I lost a buddy overseas. He died right in front of me."

The plain words, spoken so evenly, knifed Casey's heart. This was the thing. This was what brought unexplained sadness to his demeanor, a haunted look that had come over him at odd times. She'd always suspected he was holding something away from her, but she'd never imagined what it might be. "I'm sorry."

"He was a good guy. Good husband. Good dad. A better guy than I was." His fingers tightened around hers. "It should have been me."

Casey tugged her hand from his, his sadness seeping into her. No matter what had happened between them, life without him was unimaginable. Reaching for him, she laid her palms on his cheeks and turned his face toward her. "Don't."

His eyes met hers with a blue fire that stole her breath and saw straight into her soul, burning away the lies she'd been telling herself. With a clarity Casey couldn't deny, she knew. As hard as she'd tried, she hadn't been able to rip him from her heart. As much as it wasn't good for her, she still loved him. More today than the day he'd walked out of her apartment for the last time.

With a gasp, she dropped her hands and turned away from the intensity of his gaze, trying to will her body into a normal rhythm. This couldn't happen.

Besides, this wasn't about her. As much as she wanted to make it so, it wasn't. This was all about him. Her focus had to be on his needs, since he was finally baring his soul. "It shouldn't have been you." She wanted to take his hand again but didn't dare.

Travis was quiet so long she wondered if he'd somehow passed out from exhaustion in the middle of his story, but then he drew a deep breath and searched her face, his gaze tracing to her lips then up again before he looked away. "I need to check the house. Make sure everything's secure." Without any further explanation, he stood and yanked open the door, disappearing into the night.

He owed Casey an apology. Stowing his Maglite under the seat of his truck, he slammed the door and stared at the light filtering through the curtains at the kitchen window. He shouldn't have launched into a story he knew she'd never understand and he'd never finish.

And she never should have looked at him the way she had, her hands soft on his face, expression intense with something he couldn't read. Shock, maybe. Fear. Or something else… Something way too close to the way she'd looked at him when they'd sat in this very house and first talked about the future they might have. A future he'd known all along he couldn't give her. But he'd allowed himself to dream with her, of what it might be like to stay in the job he loved and to marry the woman who'd captured him at the first hello. That night, he'd felt closer to being whole than ever before, experiencing a settled happiness that he still liked to revisit on nights when he couldn't sleep, to remind himself that there was some good still in this world, even if he couldn't actually have it in his life.

It had been wrong of him then, and bringing her here had been wrong of him tonight, even though it was the only place he could think of to hide her. The moment he'd faced her and seen the compassion in her expression, he'd wanted to kiss her. To take in the part of her that was alive and joyful, the part that made him forget how fleeting everything was.

So he'd fled. All he'd wanted was a few hours in a place where no one would think to look for them. It was true they'd both have to return to work tomorrow, so this safety was all an illusion, but it was an illusion he'd thought he needed.

Turned out, illusions could be dangerous.

He'd spent half an hour in the rapidly cooling night, pacing around the house before he was satisfied they were safe and he felt like he could face her and give her the truth he should have given her months ago. His life was not his own. It was a penance paid for another man's death. Resigned to confessing everything, he trudged up the creaking wood steps and shoved open the door, braced for her questions.

Instead, Casey lay stretched out on the old leather sofa, one hand tucked under her cheek, sound asleep.

With her face peaceful, away from the stress of the past few days and the pain he'd caused her, he could almost imagine this was how she'd looked as a child, sleeping here while her great-grandfather worked in the yard or puttered around the house.

He could tell from the way she'd acted when they walked in the door that her thoughts had drifted to the same place as his. Being here brought the bittersweet ache for what they might have had in this very house.

As lightly as he could, he crossed the creaking floor and slipped the afghan from the back of the sofa, crouching to lay the covering gently across her. His arms ached for the what-might-have-been of the moment.

The realization rocked him on his heels. He still wanted Casey for the rest of his life. Whether it was right or not. Whether it fit with what he knew he had to do or not, he still wanted to belong to her for the rest of his days. The longing overrode everything else until it was all he could think about.

But soon she'd move on with her life. And when she did, it might be the thing that finally broke him.

Sinking to his knees, he rested his head on the edge of the sofa. *Lord, what is it You want me to do?* For the first time, he was silent, not simply crying out but listening, really listening. His own thoughts were too loud for him to hear if God had anything to say.

With an ache in his chest, Travis acknowledged the truth. He still loved Casey. Had never stopped loving her. For months, he'd lied to himself, afraid of the fear he felt every time he thought of the future, focused on a goal driven by another man's death.

Loving her didn't change what he had to do, didn't change the fact his future couldn't include her.

Dropping his head to the sofa by her hand, he prayed. For her to be happy. For himself when he left her. For Deacon...

A soft sound jolted him with a start. Somehow, impossibly, he'd fallen asleep with his head on the couch and his knees bent beneath him. Shaking his head, Travis eased away from the couch to keep from waking Casey and checked his watch. After three. It had been a long time since he'd slept in such a crazy position, and his knees protested as he stood with his head cocked to the side, listening.

Maybe he'd imagined it.

Travis scrubbed his hands down the sides of his face, wide awake. Falling asleep now would be impossible, unless he checked outside first to be sure.

Edging across the room to keep the floor from creaking, he stood close to the back door, hand on the knob, listening. The sound came again, a slight knock and a soft scrape, not from where he stood, but from the front of the house.

Muscles tensing for a possible fight, Travis crossed the kitchen and into the den, shutting the door between the two rooms softly behind him and cloaking the room in darkness. It was likely an animal or the wind, and the last thing Casey needed was to be startled awake by him creeping around the house. It was easy to tell from the dark circles and the lines around her eyes she hadn't had much sleep lately, probably lying awake at night same as he did.

Backlit by the soft glow from the pole light in the

side yard, a shadow crossed in front of the sheer curtains of the window beside the front door.

Someone was outside. Travis stiffened, hot anger coursing through him. Keeping close to the wall to conceal his movements as much possible, he skirted the room and stopped at the front window, lifting the curtain enough to get a clear view of the porch.

A man, dressed in jeans and a familiar dark hoodie, stood at the top of the porch steps, eyeing the front door and bouncing on his toes as though he were debating the best way to get through it.

Well, Travis would make it easy for him. In one swift motion, he turned the dead bolt and jerked the door open.

The man twitched and stumbled backward, teetering on the top step of the low porch.

Travis needed nothing more. Crouching low, he hurled himself at the would-be intruder, driving his shoulder into the man's stomach and throwing him to the ground on his back with a thud.

The other man's body cushioned the fall, but the awkward angle sent Travis to the side. He rolled onto his shoulder and rose to one knee as his opponent scrambled backward, hood dropping and exposing his face to the light from the yard lamp.

Recognition blew an image through his mind, but the memory was fleeting, slipping through his grasp. Somehow, from somewhere, he knew this guy. Not in passing, but he had spoken to him. The when and where eluded him, and as the man backed farther away, white-hot anger surged in Travis. It didn't matter who he was; he'd come after Casey. There was a price to pay.

Both men got to their feet at the same time, sizing

each other up. Travis scanned his face, trying to remember, looking for a vulnerability.

The other guy telegraphed his next move. His eyes slid to Travis's jaw as his right shoulder drew back.

With a slight smile, Travis threw out his arm and blocked the blow, the missed punch giving Travis time to land a punch of his own, square in the jaw, driving his opponent backward.

They faced off again, but this time, without warning, the man swung around with his foot and caught Travis in the shoulder, knocking him backward into the porch post, driving the air from his lungs so hard he saw stars.

It was the advantage the other man needed. He was gone around the corner of the house before Travis could recover.

Fighting for air, Travis gave chase, but the man disappeared into the woods. A few seconds later, the sound of a car drifted over from the road.

Travis smacked his palm against the porch railing. He should have been more vigilant. Should never have fallen asleep on the job. He'd left Casey vulnerable, and he'd nearly let whoever the almost-familiar man was get the upper hand.

This was why he had to shelve his feelings. Because until this was all over, he couldn't let himself lose the edge he needed to keep Casey alive.

# TWELVE

Casey held her breath for a beat, the muggy scent of an early Carolina near dawn perfumed with dew and damp leaves. She let her eyes slip closed, exhaling slowly and reveling in the soft air on her arms. Fitting the notch of the arrow into the bowstring, she raised it as one with her great-grandfather's bow. Engaging the muscles in her back, she drew the string until it touched the corner of her mouth and ignored the twinge in her shoulder. She sighted the target tacked to a hay bale across the clearing and slackened the hold in her fingers, letting the arrow fly, not releasing her stance until the arrow pierced the target slightly to the left of center.

Lowering the bow, she evaluated her aim, reset another arrow and shot again, this time landing closer to the bull's-eye.

A smile tipped her mouth and, for the first time in days, she truly believed the world wasn't fully evil. This was where she felt the most at peace. This was what her mind had been aching for since she'd first spotted Travis in the restaurant. The one thing she was good at. The one thing that never let her down.

This quiet moment before the day started, with her bow and her God.

Of course, this peace couldn't last long. She'd retrieved the old bow from the storage room and slipped out of the house early this morning, tiptoeing around the kitchen table where Travis slept with his head resting on one sprawled arm, dead to the world from exhaustion.

After he walked out last night, leaving his pain hanging in the air, she'd determined to wait for him but had succumbed to the kind of sleep she hadn't had in days. Home did this to her. And learning even a shadow of his truth and opening herself to her own had left a peace inside her she hadn't even known she was seeking.

Now, in a clearing in the trees at the back of the yard, she found the one place she knew she'd be able to grab a little bit of solitude, even if it was short-lived. Sooner or later, she'd have to return to a world flying apart.

It felt as if she had been in continuous contact with people for weeks, tugged in fifteen different directions. Not even left alone to sleep in her own apartment, dragged away from civilization on a whim... Sure, it had been only a few days, but the pressure bore down and left her wanting to burrow into a hole, not be forced into socialization.

She needed time alone to process the cascade of information and emotions that had poured over her the past few days. Needed everybody to stop hovering over her.

Well, all of it stopped tonight. Tonight, she returned

to her own apartment, danger or not. She was tired of running.

And after work, she'd go to the hospital to see Deacon one more time. Casey had debated what to say, but since the bomb he'd dropped Saturday afternoon, she'd felt some sense of responsibility, even though she couldn't quite say why. They'd talked at length over the course of several interviews about his recovery, the organizations that had helped him, the friend who'd offered advice and a listening ear... Deacon had been determined to stay clean, so what had happened to send him off the rails so far he'd overdosed?

Bracing her hand on the split-rail fence, Casey lifted her face toward heaven and sought the One who always listened, praying for Deacon and Gwen, for Travis, for John's family, for the horror to end right now so life could return to normal.

And she prayed for her heart not to break when Travis left for selection. He was focused on his career and scared of any kind of outside commitment. Even though he'd been close the past few days and had opened up the slightest bit to her last night, he wasn't going to deviate from his path and she wouldn't ask him to. *Lord, please. Take away what I'm feeling for him.*

When no relief came, she fitted yet another arrow, drew back, sighted and let fly, a little more of the tension she held in her aching shoulders releasing into the arrow as it slammed the target.

Dead center.

Bull's-eye.

The full-blown grin on her face faded when a low whistle floated from behind her.

Casey whirled, heart racing.

Stupid. She'd come out here alone knowing someone was on the prowl and now she'd have to face whoever had followed her without anyone to back her up.

The intruder standing near the house was a greater danger than anyone who might be targeting them. Travis stood about thirty feet away, leaning against a tree at the edge of the clearing, arms crossed over his chest. He was dressed for the duty day, his uniform making him appear taller and broader than usual.

Something twinged in her chest, and it was not a thing she'd call good. *Lord, we just talked about this. Just. Talked. About. This.* Wasn't there a verse somewhere in the Bible about not being tempted beyond what she could bear?

Travis tipped his head toward the target, looking past her. "Nice shot. You've gotten better since the last time we were out here."

We. Like they'd planned this outing together this morning. Well, they hadn't, and he could leave now, before she said something she shouldn't.

Instead, Travis straightened and strode closer, his bearing tall, his attitude sure.

Man, she needed to quit noticing him. Every time they were together, he drew her in more. Casey couldn't look away from him as he came closer, and it was a fight to ignore the way her stomach fluttered and tugged at a heart still raw from realizing how she really felt.

He stopped mere inches away, the smell of soap mingling with the morning breeze, a strong reminder of all the times she'd been next to him in the past, when they'd talked, when he'd held her close, when he'd kissed her.

She let her eyes drift to his lips, where they lingered for a tantalizing breath before she planted them squarely on the rank on his chest.

Yeah, that was the past. He'd moved on.

She needed to.

"You should have let me know you were coming out here." Travis stopped himself and shoved his hands into the front pockets of his uniform pants. "I guess you needed a break, huh?"

Casey's eyebrows drew together. She held the bow low at her side and backed away enough to breathe without inhaling the scent that would always be his alone. "The walls were closing in." Her words held a tone of challenge she didn't feel, but really, she was daring him to do something to push her away. Or daring him to finish what he'd started last night and pull her to him. She wasn't sure which.

"Freaked me out a little bit when I woke up and you were gone." His voice dipped, husky and intimate. "But I knew exactly where you'd be." He reached out and ran his fingers down the bow at her side, a slight smile softening his features. "Your great-grandfather's. You tried to teach me and I was miserable at it."

The words washed over her like a warm blanket, easing the tension in her shoulders but tightening something in her abdomen, something she hadn't felt since the first time he'd kissed her. Anticipation, excitement…

Her breath caught in her throat. No. No. No. She didn't need this. He was here because he felt some twisted need to protect her. Nothing more. In a week, he'd be gone, off to selection, moving forward with his career and leaving her behind with feelings he could never return.

But standing here in front of him, she couldn't turn away. All she felt was hope. Stupid, peace-destroying hope that he'd look at her again and see how much she loved him, and maybe he still loved her, too. More likely hope would crush her when he walked away.

She had to say something to break whatever this moment was layering between them. Casey lifted her chin and looked over his shoulder toward the house. "You could have called me from the porch. I'd have heard you."

He didn't turn his attention from her. Even though she wasn't looking directly at him, Casey could tell he was still watching her.

"I didn't want to disturb you and, I guess…" He sidestepped to stand next to her, his shoulder warm against hers as he stared at the target.

What a perfect picture for what their relationship had been, side by side, facing two different directions.

He sniffed and stood taller. "I wanted to give you your space. But then I saw you… I don't know, there's something about watching you do what you love. I didn't want to interrupt when I might not get the chance to see you doing this ever again."

Her pulse jumped. He'd wanted to see her outside of everything happening between them, but he wasn't hanging around. He never would.

"Case, I knew you needed to get away this morning. And I know part of the reason you're stressed is…me." Something deep in his voice tore at her.

The words jolted through her. He couldn't know. He

could never know. "You have a pretty high opinion of yourself, don't you? I mean, John's dead, Deacon's in the hospital, somebody tried to—"

He turned toward her, his chest grazing her shoulder as his fingers brushed a strand of hair behind her ear, and stopped her words. "I get it. All of it. Maybe what I should have said was I'm stressed about you. I passed out sitting at the table last night because every night before it has been a wreck because all I can think about is…"

*You.*

That couldn't be what he was about to say. Her pulse galloped, the hope she'd tried to quench flaming into life. If he didn't stop now, she'd tell him everything she'd come to realize.

And once again, Travis Heath would make a fool of her when he told her he didn't feel the same.

Something in Casey's expression shifted, and she turned away from him. "Travis, don't."

He exhaled loudly, dropping his hand to his side with a dull thud. Somehow, he was wrecking this and he didn't know how to fix it. Everything inside him wanted to tell her what he'd realized last night. He loved her. He needed her. But he couldn't. Not when he was about to walk away from her. And definitely not when he'd been so focused on her that he'd let a man nearly sneak right past him.

Then fallen into a dead sleep as dawn peeked over the horizon. Sleep brought on by too many nights lying awake and thinking about Casey Jordan. Still, he had to tell her something.

"I needed to say that what I did, walking away from

you… It was wrong. And it wasn't even what I really wanted." He dragged a hand through his hair. "I don't even know for sure anymore what I want except not to hurt you."

Casey turned and went toe-to-toe with him, letting her gaze drill into his. "Well, you failed. It hurts."

He flinched. "I'm sorry."

Casey's jaw slackened, her eyes widening. Clearly, she'd been expecting anything else.

He'd said it. He'd apologized. So why didn't he feel any better?

Because *I'm sorry* was only the thing he wanted to *say*. What he wanted to *do* was entirely different.

Casey was so close, Travis could smell the apple in her shampoo and almost count the brown flecks in her gray eyes. Somehow it felt as if shielding her from the bad around them would protect him, too. Like it would make the darkness creeping in on him fade into the corners of the world.

Casey Jordan made him a better man. Beside her, he felt taller. He felt capable, like he could overcome all the things he'd seen overseas, even the blood and the death he'd never really, on a deep level, talked to anyone about, not even her.

On the night Travis had left Casey, Phil had said he was better off without her, and healing would be easier on both of them. In this moment, Travis knew Phil was wrong. Because since he'd walked away three months ago, his whole life had skewed, and the black of his memories crept ever closer, threatening to swallow him.

Her eyes never left his, and he knew the intensity of his thoughts showed on his face. That was probably why she was staring at him, frozen, as though she were trapped in whatever he was thinking right along with him.

His gaze roamed from her eyes, to her lips, to the small scar she'd gotten when she'd released a bow string too close to her cheek and sliced the delicate skin. It was her lone imperfection.

Lifting his hand, he traced the scar with his thumb, wishing he could take away the hurt he'd caused, needing a way to tell her his thoughts but not quite able to say what had slapped him senseless as he'd watched her sleep last night. Since he'd seen her in the restaurant with John, and Deacon had fired the cryptic warning he'd kept from Casey, his feelings for her had grown stronger until they threatened to swamp him.

Casey swallowed hard and her breath caught in her throat, her lips moving as if she were going to say something but couldn't.

He couldn't resist her anymore. He slipped his palm against her cheek and eased along the soft skin of her neck into her hair, pulling her near, pressing his forehead against hers, close enough for her breath to brush his lips. He'd never thought he'd be this close to her again. For one precious second, he hovered in heartstopping anticipation.

There was no more fight left. Travis brushed a whisper of a kiss across the scar on her cheek, then sought her lips and found them, letting go of everything in his entire world but the woman before him.

She met him fully, slipping her arms around his waist and drawing him closer.

His hands wound deeper in her hair, trying to get as close to her as possible, to communicate his emotions in a way his words couldn't. Everything else slipped away and there was nothing but this woman, filling all his senses and awakening every dead place inside him.

He was going to drown in her if he didn't come up for air.

Travis pulled away slightly, brushed a kiss beside her eye, then held her tight against him, pressing his cheek into her hair and taking in the scent of her. Right now, he could give up everything else and ask her for the rest of her life. They could work the rest out as they went. He could do it all, as long as she was with him.

Slowly, Casey slipped her arms from his back and brought her hands between them, pressing against his chest.

He resisted at first, then let her ease a few inches away.

She stayed in the circle of his arms, her cheek pressed against her hands on his chest as though she wanted to break away but couldn't find the strength.

Pressing a kiss to her temple, Travis dug deep for a way to tell her what was on his heart and to say the words he'd almost said before.

The words he should have said before.

But he couldn't. If he said them, he could never take them back, not without hurting her even worse than he had the first time. His life wasn't his own, and he couldn't promise her a future when he could die on any given deployment. The way things were shaping up around them now, either of them could die right here on home soil. The thought pulsed through him, hot and paralyzing.

Casey had to sense his tension. She stiffened and slipped out of his embrace. "I can't do this."

The softly spoken words were a blow. "Casey, I—"

"You're not sure what you want, even now. Getting over you was… No, I'm not over you. But I can't let you pull me in and then shove me away again. You don't get to do that. I won't let you." Without ever lifting her head, she slipped around him and walked away.

Hot shame washed over Travis, heating him from the inside out as Casey disappeared into the trees that hid the farmhouse from view.

Travis's shoulders sagged. His muscles strained to chase her and tell her he loved her and there was a way to work this out.

But as the distance grew between them, so did the certainty her walking away was the right thing. He'd hurt her before, and he'd have to let her go and let God take his time healing her.

And he needed a lot more time with God, because his future grew muddier with every moment he spent in Casey's presence.

# THIRTEEN

Travis scrubbed his hand across his forehead, still damp from physical training. He stood in the quad at the battalion and watched soldiers filter out to grab showers and hot chow. He ought to follow them—his stomach urged him hard—but he couldn't. Instead of taking care of himself, he planned to use this brief bit of free time to drive by Public Affairs and make sure Casey was safe.

He couldn't shake the thought he wasn't doing enough. Not only was someone coming at them from the outside, he'd ripped her apart on the inside. Travis kicked at the ground, frustrated by his own double mind. "This grass needs to be cut, Luke. Can't they find somebody who needs a little extra discipline to get on this mess?"

Behind him, Lucas laughed. "Are you seriously about to go all Martha Stewart about the grass around the battalion?"

"Maybe."

"This isn't about the grass, man. It's about you wishing you were across post instead of here." The knowing sheen over Lucas's words was almost too much. Like he knew how Travis was feeling right now. Like he'd ever had to sit helplessly by while the woman he loved dodged danger.

Then again, he was probably one of the few people who knew exactly what Travis was feeling. Last year, Lucas had spent whole nights camped out on his front porch, keeping an eye on Kristin's house when someone threatened her, denying the whole time he was in love with her.

It had been Travis who'd harassed him until he admitted it. He rolled his eyes skyward then turned to face Lucas, who was standing about ten feet away. "Payback is a beast, huh?"

"Not for me. I'm the one dishing it out."

"Right."

"Get your feet moving so we can grab some chow. I'm hungry. I'll even let you drive by Casey's office on the way." Lucas started walking toward the company, the grin slipping from his face. "You know, you never should have let her go. Of all the dumb things you've done, leaving her was—"

"Don't start." Hammering away at his stupidity after the fact was pointless. Yeah, he'd let Casey go. He'd chosen his career over her when she hadn't even given him an ultimatum. He was paying for it all now in a firestorm of confusion and uncertainty, the flames extra high after watching her walk away this morning.

"You realize I saved your life after that." Lucas's voice lifted with a tinge of amusement. "I had to almost physically keep Kristin from coming after you and giving you a need for reconstructive surgery."

Travis choked on a laugh. He didn't doubt it. Lucas's fiancée was the toughest woman he'd ever met, and she was a fierce defender of the ones she loved.

His amusement took a dive straight into his running shoes. Travis had hurt her best friend. He wouldn't have argued if Kristin had come at him. He'd have deserved it. Still did. It was a little bit surprising she hadn't marched across the street the other night and given him a piece of her mind, three months after the fact.

"Sooner or later," Lucas said, "you're going to have to quit running scared."

"Scared?" Now he was pushing it a little bit too far. Stopping as they reached the sidewalk, Travis crossed his arms and leveled his best platoon sergeant glare on his buddy. "The only thing I was afraid of was hurting her."

"Of being happy."

Travis arched an eyebrow and dug his fingers into his biceps. He didn't get mad often, and almost never at Lucas, but right now the pin on the grenade was dangerously close to slipping out.

"Don't look at me like you're going to punch me in the face. I can take you, Heath." Lucas stopped walking and held up a hand to keep Travis from speaking. "You act like you're Mr. Fun-and-Games, but you're covering this fear that if you let yourself be happy, it will all get snatched away because you somehow don't deserve it. I get it. Your family lost everything when you were a kid. You watched a buddy die right in front of you. Kristin's brother was taken out by a shot he never saw coming. Sure, any of us could die at any second, but you can't live your whole life afraid."

"Knock it off." Lucas had zero idea of what he was talking about.

"You're next to impossible." Lucas threw up his hands, his voice hard. "What was it you said to me once? 'If it's my time, it's my time. Any of us could die sitting on the couch just as likely as in a war zone.' Those words came out of your mouth."

If he'd ever said such a thing, he must have been out of his head.

"You know, we're all going to die someday. All of us. But God never intended any of us to live like we're already dead."

Travis clenched his fists and leveled Lucas with a glare, anger blowing hot through his very soul. "You keep talking and you're going to have to back up what you're saying with—"

"With what? What are you going to do? Throw a punch? You wouldn't. I know you. You think you're angry right now, but it's not anger. It's fear. You're so tied in knots you don't even know who you are anymore."

"And you don't know what you're saying. It wasn't death I was afraid of when I broke it off with Casey." Though it sure was now.

"I think, deep down, it was. The death of that relationship. You were scared it would end one day, so you made it end on your terms. And another thing... You're still alive. Your buddy isn't. I get it. But somewhere you came up with this twisted idea God wants you to live a life full of penance, and you've got some calling that demands everything you've got. You need to ease up on yourself. Talk to God and see if it's His voice you're hearing or if it's survivor guilt doing a number on you. I let it go when you dumped Sergeant

Wilson's sister right before we deployed, because she wasn't right for you. Casey, on the other hand…"

Travis dropped his gaze. He'd apologized to Lisa Wilson, and she'd forgiven him. But the fallout had cost him the respect of her brother, one of the other platoon sergeants. It had taken a lot to ease the tension between them overseas, especially since Wilson had warned his sister Travis was the kind of guy to love 'em and leave 'em. In those days, he'd been a hard-living, hard-partying, stereotypical soldier. But then along came Lucas. His Ranger buddy and fellow platoon sergeant had backed Travis against the wall and made him face himself. Made him face the God who had been chasing Travis a lot longer than he'd cared to admit.

Lucas was right. Casey was different. He'd found himself feeling things for her he'd never felt before, feelings that were growing stronger if this morning was any indication. But he'd left her anyway, in a blazing haze of fear that he'd turn around one day and she'd be gone. Not because she'd died but because she'd figured out the fraud he was and left him.

Maybe Lucas was right.

And he wasn't finished yet. "You blew a good thing, Heath. We're not going to pretend you didn't. And you blew it the same way I almost did with Kristin. Because you were believing a lie. Still are."

Travis couldn't take any more words pounding into his head. None of it made sense. All of it made him question what he thought he knew, and now wasn't the time, not with Casey in danger. Not with him having no idea where the next shot could come from. Going through some kind of pseudotherapy with Lucas wasn't helping anybody do anything. "You know what? It's not for you to decide. Besides, with everything happening right now, starting anything with Casey is out of the question." Even though he almost had this morning. He still wondered if he should have stopped her from walking away and scrapped the rest of his life plans, especially now with Lucas hammering on him about truth and guilt and God.

Lucas stomped up the steps and jerked the door open. "Know what? You're stubborn and blind. Might be time for you to stop talking so much to God and start listening to what He's trying to tell you."

Casey's fingers rested on the keyboard, her thumbs twitching on the space bar. The absolute conformity of the office—cream concrete walls, sparse military furnishings, plaques and awards—usually brought order and peace to her world. Today, the walls closed in and all she wanted to do was pack her bags and run away, as far as she could get. There had to be somewhere safe from unknown threats, drug overdoses and death. And from Travis Heath.

All the peace she'd found when her arrow landed on the bull's-eye this morning had evaporated with Travis's kiss. True, he'd kissed her before, but this time something else rocked her backward with its intensity. For the first time, he'd kissed her as though he was giving her everything, with a force that met her own feelings and magnified them until they almost knocked her off her feet.

Then his entire emotional state had shifted. She'd felt it all the way through her. He'd walled himself off.

She wasn't going there with him again.

Letting him get close had been a mistake, and this

morning had driven the point home. She'd almost lost herself right there. Nearly gave up everything in her life to safety in his arms. But that wasn't safety. It was a fleeting moment before he came to his senses and bolted yet again, chased by the death of a soldier he felt responsible for.

At least now she knew why he'd cut her the way he had. His apology had blindsided her. She'd always assumed he was callous to her pain.

Then, when he'd kissed her, she'd been overwhelmed by everything she'd ever believed *home* would be. Peace, safety, comfort… The settledness of being exactly where she wanted and needed to be forever.

Except that couldn't be right, because he wasn't capable of giving her all of himself.

So she'd run.

What she wouldn't give for Sergeant Brenner to come by and ask her for the usual cup of coffee, but his presence was conspicuously absent this morning, the large room quieter than normal without his teasing voice. It was probably for the best. This morning if he asked her out, she might say yes, if only to spite her own crazy emotions. It wouldn't be fair to him or to herself.

Casey crossed her arms on her desk and dropped her head to stare into nothingness. She popped right back up again when the morning started its unending replay in the dark. Forget it. She shook her shoulders and focused on the computer screen in front of her.

She had work to do. Deep inside, where her intuition spoke loudest, she knew there was more to come. If either of them were going to get out of this unscathed, she had to find answers.

The run to the farm last night had left Casey with more questions. Deacon's confession to her had tickled something in her mind, something John had said when she'd interviewed him for the addiction article, but the memory wouldn't quite come to the forefront. Several months ago, she'd recorded the conversation and transcribed the notes she needed, then she'd never touched them again. If John had told her something she wasn't supposed to know, maybe the answers were in her files after all.

Logging into her cloud account, she clicked to the folder containing her interviews and opened the one from the first time she and John had talked.

Work. Focus on work and keep Travis and blood-stained memories at bay.

Scanning the notes, she stopped at one John had later asked her not to use. During their conversation, he'd talked about coming home from his first deployment, when he'd been assigned to Fort Bragg shortly after his return. Battling his memories, he'd started drinking heavily and confided to a new friend he was struggling. The notes stopped there. She remembered the conversation and wishing he had let her use it, but he'd seemed to think it was better left unwritten.

Casey scrolled through her files until she found the recording of the session and played it, the voice of a dead man sending shivers along her arms. If she could find the truth here, she might help John point the finger at his own killer.

Whoever the "friend" was, he'd been helpful at first, but then he'd turned John toward a designer drug that offered an escape but left him with a wicked addiction. He'd used for months, then come to his senses and sought help.

Toward the end of the conversation, John seemed to forget he was talking to her. His voice took on the quality of memory tinged with regret. "Guy who used to be my team leader introduced me to him. He lives out near Raeford. Big piece of property. Lots of space. Pretty persuasive, too. I trusted him, especially since his wife's…" A long pause dominated the recording, then he cleared his throat and chuckled. "Know what? We can leave that part out."

A soft tap on her cubicle stopped her from hearing any more.

Deacon's fiancée, Gwen, stood next to her cubicle, waiting uncertainly.

Casey stood, a tremor jolting through her. If Deacon's fiancée was here in person, it could only mean…

Gwen must have read Casey's thoughts on her face, because she leaned closer and laid a hand on Casey's arm. "Deacon's fine."

With an exhale Gwen was bound to be able to hear, Casey sank into her seat and pointed at a chair wedged next to her desk. "Please." She waited for Gwen to settle in. "How's he doing? Any word yet on when he'll get to go home?"

"He's a roller coaster. This should have been a fast turnaround, but I don't know. He relapsed last night after you and Travis left, but there's no way he got his hands on more drugs. Docs can't figure it out. But if he has a good day today, they should be releasing him this time tomorrow." Gwen hung her purse on the arm of the chair. "And I didn't mean to scare you coming here without calling first."

"I'm sorry. I thought when I saw you that you were bringing more bad news in person."

"More bad news?" Gwen's sculpted eyebrow arched. "Has something else happened?"

"A whole lot of somethings, but none of it has to do with Deacon or you." At least, she hoped not. "What can I do for you?"

"I don't know." Gwen's lips pressed together until the corners nearly turned white against her dark skin. "I know you interviewed Deacon before about addiction and recovery and I thought... I'm prior service and knew a lot of people who looked to crazy stuff to deal with what they'd seen. I didn't know if you'd be willing to work on another story about..." She shook her head and offered a forced smile. "Watching Deacon suffer makes me want to do something, and I thought you could help. It's part of the reason I'm here today."

"Okay." The hairs along Casey's arms raised. She couldn't quite say why, but something about Gwen's demeanor and her words left her uneasy, almost like Travis's expression earlier. There was more to both of their stories than they were saying. "Tell me how I can help."

"I wanted you to know, first off, as far as I know Deacon was clean for a long time. Several years. He's not talking to me about when he started back or how, just says he never should have started hanging out with John again. John's the one who was supplying him. Funny thing is, though—" Gwen sat forward in the chair "—I can't think of any signs to say he was using again. He's been the same guy all along. So unless he's been lying to me for years, he relapsed recently. Very, very recently."

"Are you sure he'd want me to write about this?"

"I don't know. I wanted to talk to you first. He doesn't even know I'm here."

"Might be something you want to discuss with him."

"I will. Eventually." Gwen deflated in the chair, her forehead creased. "There's something else. Before Deacon landed in the hospital, we saw on the news where someone killed John. That was one of the reasons he wanted to talk to you the other day, but then he acted like he regretted saying something."

Casey nodded once. The news had run the story of the murder without giving any details about the beating beforehand. No need to tip their hand.

She fought a shudder. It would be nice if she could be as ignorant as the rest of the area about the state of John's body when he died.

Reaching down, Gwen pulled a small folded piece of paper from her purse and passed it to Casey. "I don't know much about this but maybe you do."

Casey unfolded the paper and read the hastily scrawled words written there. *Ketamine. Fentanyl.* "These two came up in the story I interviewed Deacon for the first time. They're drugs used for sedation or pain relief. Fairly common. Ketamine especially has found its way to the streets as a recreational drug. An overdose of either one can slow heart rate and respiration down to dangerous levels."

"That's what happened to Deacon."

Casey's fingers closed tighter around the paper. "He's using these?" Ketamine especially was tricky. What might drop one man into extreme sedation could kill another. That kind of unpredictability might have saved Deacon's life.

"I don't know, but it's what almost killed him. Some-body got him in the neck when he was leaving his apartment. The docs checked. There's a mark, a small one, right by his jugular."

The hair on Casey's arms stood, a cold wave running through her. First John at his house, then Deacon… "Somebody tried to kill him." Which meant someone was definitely after the team, and Travis could be in greater danger than she'd thought. Casey wanted to run to her Jeep and press the pedal to the floor to get to Travis and warn him things were growing worse by the second.

Gwen's mouth was set in a grim line. "It looks like Deacon was targeted. And when the doctors checked his system, those two drugs are what they found." For the first time, she grew bold enough to look Casey in the eye. "The two of you went looking for him, and if you hadn't, whoever wanted him dead would have suc-ceeded. They didn't. So both of us owe you."

Casey dropped her hands into her lap and dug her fingernails into her palms. No, these shadow people hadn't succeeded in taking out Deacon on their first attempt. But John's death still haunted her waking and sleeping thoughts, and there was no doubt that since whoever had tried to kill Deacon had failed, they would definitely try again. She shoved away from her desk and stood. "Who's with Deacon now?"

"When I left, there was a police officer there. He wanted me to step out while they spoke, so I thought it was a good time for me to come and talk to you. Why?" Fear edged Gwen's question. "What do you think is going on?"

"I think Deacon's still in danger and shouldn't be

alone." Casey grabbed her cell phone as she shoved away from her desk and searched her recent calls, looking for Travis's number. She stopped and looked at Gwen. "Follow me to the hospital." *And pray we're not too late.*

# FOURTEEN

"Jankowski, tell me one more time." Travis sat in his chair and looked at the young private standing in front of his desk. Some things would never make sense, including young soldiers and some of their weekend antics. Even though the man in front of him had acted like he had no sense of his own, at least the momentary diversion kept Travis from thinking what an idiot he'd been with Casey this morning.

He shoved the thought from his mind and focused on his soldier. Kid had probably never been in trouble before. He was squared away but young and still a little bit invincible.

Behind Jankowski, Lucas sat at the platoon leader's desk waiting for Travis to wrap up so they could go to lunch, but Travis knew better than to look at him. The tension that had built between them earlier had dissipated with the absurdity of the moment, and both of them would start laughing like a couple of high school kids. "How is it you lost your car? Not your bicycle or your skateboard or even your keys. Your car. It's not like you could shove it in your pocket or leave it on a bar somewhere."

Private Jankowski stared at a spot over Travis's head. "I don't know. It's like I told my squad leader, it's just gone. It was in a parking lot downtown, and now it's gone."

Travis propped his elbow on the chair and gripped his chin, wishing he had time to mess with the kid a little bit more, but his phone had vibrated about five times in his breast pocket, so it had to be somebody needing him pretty badly.

He said a quick prayer nothing had happened to Casey. His fingers itched to check, but he couldn't until he'd finished his job. "You know, Private, I can't see your future or anything, but I hear things, and I can promise you this. You keep drinking the way you've been drinking, and you're going to lose a whole lot more than your car."

Jankowski started to speak, but Travis didn't give him the chance. "Don't bother telling me you were sober last night. You weren't. I already know. Nobody sober loses a vehicle. The saving grace for you is you lost it so you didn't drive it. Get behind the wheel after a night like you clearly had last night and you won't want to be seeing me the next day, you hearing me?"

Nodding once, Jankowski let his gaze bounce to Travis's then to the wall above his head, ready to get out of the room. No telling why. He'd hit the hallway and have to endure the verbal hazing his buddies certainly had waiting for him. This little lecture was going to be the easy part of the kid's day.

Travis aimed a finger at the door. "If I were in your shoes, I'd go find my phone and start calling tow companies. I'm going to make an educated guess one of them has your vehicle."

Without another word, Jankowski turned and left the room, making an obvious effort to keep his head high.

Lucas waited several beats before he spoke, the corner of his mouth twitching as though his amusement wasn't going to stay inside much longer. "Lost his car? Are you kidding me?"

"I wish I was." Travis yanked open the breast pocket of his uniform and jerked his phone out. "I think it's a first for me."

"Both of us did some dumb things, but I'm pretty sure neither of us lost anything as big as a vehicle." Lucas shook his head and stood, ready to get moving. "Who's so desperate to get in touch with you? I could hear your phone buzzing from here."

Travis's hand tightened on the device. "Casey." Seven missed calls from Casey, but no texts or voice mails. Deacon's warning rang like a fire alarm in his memory.

Surely not. He was jumping to conclusions. He had to be, because anything else was too much to think. Maybe she'd decided what had happened between them this morning wasn't such a bad thing after all and wanted to talk.

Doubtful. Either she was boiling mad over the way he'd kissed her or she was in trouble. Since Casey tended to have a slow burn that built over days, anger probably wasn't the answer. Something had to be desperately wrong for her to turn to him when she'd made it clear she was turning away this morning. The desk drawer squealed in protest as Travis yanked it open and grabbed his truck keys then stood, pressing the screen to return her call.

Across the room, Lucas pulled his maroon beret

from his leg pocket, preparing to follow Travis wherever he was headed. "What's going on?"

"I don't know." He held the phone to his ear as it rang until voice mail kicked in, then cut the call and tried again. "She's not answering." Standing beside his desk, he squeezed his keys tighter, digging the jagged edges into his palm. He was helpless, unable to go anywhere or do anything without knowing where she was.

His past failures weighed on him. He couldn't miss the cues again. Not now. *Come on, Casey. Answer.*

Lucas was at attention, as ready to get moving as Travis. "Want me to call Kristin?"

Pressing the screen to shut off the sound of Casey's voice mail, Travis nodded once. "Can't hurt. I'm going to her office to—" The phone vibrated in his palm and nearly fell from his hand.

He glanced at the screen. Casey. Holding the phone to his ear, he strode for the door. "Are you safe? Where are you?"

"Headed to the hospital."

His heartbeat quickened and he practically ran out the office door, Lucas close on his heels. "What happened?"

"Nothing yet. But things aren't good." The more she talked about Deacon's condition, the faster Travis walked.

"Ketamine and fentanyl?" Travis stopped at the door that exited the company building and glanced around to make sure no one was in the immediate area. With lunch having started a couple of minutes ago, all the soldiers had vanished until one. He tilted the phone so Lucas could hear. "Fentanyl I've heard of, but what's ketamine?"

"I called a source from my addiction story to double-check. That's why I didn't answer you when you first called. It's an anesthetic. In small doses, it can cause disassociation and hallucinations and some pretty nasty side effects. High enough doses can knock somebody out. It's becoming a hot commodity with the younger crowd, pretty easy to get on the street and used in a cocktail to create designer drugs. Stolen from veterinary clinics a lot. Mixed with fentanyl in the right proportions, it's lethal."

"Definitely not something Deacon would have mixed himself unless he was suicidal."

"Exactly. I'm heading to the hospital now to make sure he's not alone. Gwen's behind me."

"No." Tugging his beret onto his head, Travis shoved through the door into the sunlight, squinting against the brightness of a Carolina noon. The last thing she needed to do was go to the very place Deacon had warned them away from. "Lie low. Call the cops and have their man stay with Deacon. Don't you dare get in the middle of this. Somebody's out for blood."

"Gwen's already called ahead and someone is with him, but somebody who knows what's going on should be there, too. Besides, I'm not the one in danger. You are. It's pretty clear now this is about your team, don't you think?"

He should have told her about what happened last night, but he'd kept it from her, trying not to add any more stress to the situation. "Stay out of this, Case." He wasn't about to risk losing her, especially not since he was figuring out exactly how much he needed her. The thought ripped through him, hot and cold at the same time.

She was quiet for a moment, but when she spoke again, her voice was firm. "A man's life is at stake."

"And so is yours." Travis yanked open the driver's door of his truck and looked across the interior at Lucas, dipping his chin toward the other man's phone. "Call the hospital. Make sure they paid attention when Gwen called and they're getting somebody to Deacon's room now." He tilted the phone speaker closer. "Casey, listen to me. There's no reason for you to go there."

"I'm going."

"Then stay in the car when you get there and wait for me."

"What can you do that I can't?"

Travis pulled his head back as though he was dodging a blow. Casey wasn't usually combative. In fact, almost never. She was either desperate because of the situation or furious with him about this morning. "I can have your back."

Her silence said everything Travis didn't want to hear. He'd failed to have her back before. Why should things be any different now?

Because he was a different man. And he wasn't letting her walk alone into danger.

# FIFTEEN

On the third level of the cramped hospital parking deck, Casey's Jeep was empty.

Travis planted his fists on his hips to keep from pounding his palm on the hood of her vehicle. He should have known she wouldn't stay put after she'd all but hung up on him earlier.

Lucas stood at the bumper of the Jeep and crossed his arms. "Looks like she didn't listen to you any more than Kristin listened to me when somebody was after her last year."

"Yeah, well, why should she?" Travis turned on one heel and strode for the stairs at the opposite corner of the parking deck, his bootfalls echoing in the concrete structure.

"Because both of you are in danger and both of you are so busy denying it and pointing fingers at each other that you can't see it." Lucas caught up and kept pace beside him. "Face it, Heath. You're as stubborn and closed minded as she is. It's no wonder things didn't work out between you."

"You can stop talking anytime." Travis burst into the stairwell and took the stairs two at a time.

"Just observing. Kind of like you did to me not too long ago."

"You mean I was this annoying?"

"Even more. You thought you were funny."

Forget it. He could stop in the stairwell, whip around on Lucas and have it out right now, but his buddy wasn't the problem. Invisible killers were the problem. Deacon's near-death experience being a violent act was the problem. Kissing Casey was the problem.

Lucas and his sarcasm were the least of Travis's worries. All he could envision was someone jerking Casey into a dark corner of the parking deck or shoving her into a dented, rusty old van like the bad guys drove in the movies. His brain was running away with him, and he couldn't make the video stop. Like those nights right after Aiken died, the replay made him want to dig his fingers into his skull and physically claw the visions out.

Exiting the deck, he forced himself not to run as he crossed to the hospital's main entrance and stepped into the air-conditioned main lobby dominated by a large welcome desk.

Thankfully, Lucas didn't push the issue and stood at the desk beside him, swiping his maroon beret from his head and tucking it into his leg pocket.

For once, there wasn't a line at security, and Travis sent up a quick prayer of thanks. He ran his hand over his hair then pulled out his wallet and passed his military ID to the security guard. "Travis Heath. I'm going to see Deacon Lewis."

The woman took the card and typed something into her computer. She stared at the screen, and her eyebrows drew together before she glanced at Travis, then to the screen again. "Deacon Lewis?"

Something as close to panic as he'd felt in a long time rammed Travis in the chest. There was too much suspicion and concern in her voice.

The phone calls Lucas and Gwen had made to the hospital had been too late. "Is Deacon okay, ma'am?"

The woman didn't look up as she slid his ID across the counter toward him with one hand and reached for the phone with the other. "I think you should talk to—"

"Travis."

He turned and brushed past Lucas, walking toward Casey's voice before he'd even fully located where it was coming from.

She stood to the side, her uniform doing very little to hide the woman she was, her mouth tight, face lined with worry.

Wanting to hold her close and knowing he shouldn't, Travis ignored the security guard calling him for a visitors pass and stopped in front of Casey.

She seemed to have shrunk in the past few hours, and her gray eyes were missing the spark he'd fallen in love with. "Deacon coded, but they were able to resuscitate him."

Somehow, he'd known the news wouldn't be good, even on the drive over when he hadn't wanted to admit it. He hurt all over for her, for Gwen, for Deacon…

Without worrying what she'd think, Travis opened his arms and invited her in.

Casey walked into his embrace, her hands pressed between them, and buried her face in his shoulder.

Closing the circle, Travis held her close in the only protection he could offer, certain he could somehow shield her from everything going on around them, believing for the first time in months she might actually still trust him.

Like he might be worthy of her trust.

She didn't cry, just sort of melted into him, as though he was the one thing that could hold her up. It didn't matter what had changed from this morning, only that right now, when she needed someone most, she'd turned to him.

Not only was she drawing on his strength, he needed hers, as well. There was a give-and-take between them he'd never felt before, his own grief mingling with hers in a whole new shared experience.

After an entirely too short time, she backed away and straightened her shoulders, nodding to Lucas then staring at the rank on Travis's chest like she couldn't quite muster the energy to lift her head.

As much as he wanted to rewind time about fifteen seconds and have her in his arms again, where they'd both been safe, this space between them was probably saving him from saying or doing something insanely stupid. "What happened?"

"Nobody's sure yet." Edging around him, she tipped her head toward the door and led Travis and Lucas outside and along the sidewalk, away from anyone who might overhear. "When Gwen came to my office this morning, she said Deacon had a rough night, almost like he'd dosed himself again, even though it would be impossible for him to get his hands on anything and no one's signed in to visit him. Then, she dropped the bombshell about him being drugged. While she was with me today, he bottomed out. They brought him around, but the doctors can't give her a reason why any of this is happening. They're running tests now."

Travis dragged a hand against his cheek, scrubbing his palm along the beginnings of a five o'clock shadow, not liking his thoughts. No matter what angle he turned this, the conclusion never changed. "Somebody with access to Deacon is afraid he's going to talk about something."

"Explain." Lucas's head tilted to the side, and he glanced around to make sure no one was near. "You think somebody is trying to silence Deacon right under the doctors' noses?"

It was a leap the size of the Grand Canyon, but with Deacon's warning ringing in his ears, it was the one thing that made sense. "He said something to me about how he and John never should have started hanging around... And then he stopped without giving me a name. There's somebody else involved for certain, and Deacon's afraid of them, even in the relative safety of the hospital. Whoever it is, they have a long reach."

Casey straightened and wrapped a hand around Travis's biceps as though she were trying to hold on to an idea before it ran from her. "I went through my notes this morning. John said almost the same thing, something about a guy who lives near Raeford, has a lot of property. Called him a friend he'd gone to for advice. The guy was dealing a designer drug, a depressant. Pretty much the same thing Deacon said when I interviewed him for the first story." She squinted, her shoulders sagging as her hand fell from Travis's arm. "But one thing doesn't make sense. Why push Deacon to the brink then pull him back last night just to nearly kill him today?"

"Threatening him?" Lucas asked.

Leaning against a small tree next to the sidewalk, Travis crossed his arms and studied the Life Flight helicopter situated on the helipad in front of the hospital. Sunlight reflected off the windows, but the brightness did nothing to shed light on his dark thoughts. "He told me not to ask any more questions. Said we'd already been warned."

Casey gasped.

Lucas cocked his head to the side, his expression hardening. "How long have you been holding on to this piece of information?"

"Last night." He couldn't look at Casey. She was probably trying to burn him to ashes with her eyeballs. "I'm guessing by 'warning' he meant what happened downtown."

"What questions were you asking?" Casey's voice was low, anger adding weight.

He should have told her earlier, but he'd thought it best to protect her from more worry and to remind her as little as possible of those last moments with John. He'd looked right at Casey as he spoke his last word, yet she had never mentioned it. It had to be something she was trying to shove out of her memory. "What John said right before he died."

When he dared to look at her, her face had paled, but she stood as tall as ever. "I knew he said something, but honestly, I was too focused on what I was seeing to hear it."

"He said 'bet.'"

Lucas squinted. "Gambling?"

"I thought so at first, but it doesn't fit. When I said it to Deacon, he acted like he knew exactly what I meant.

It's the thing that spooked him. He was talking about using, and how John and he never should have gotten involved with whoever it was—" Something Casey had said leaped up, almost visible in the air, bringing with it a suspicion he should never have. Ever. But the more he thought about it, the more those pieces he'd been fighting to wrestle together slipped into place, forming a picture he'd never imagined was coming. "Case, where did you say the guy lived that John was dealing with?"

"Raeford."

"And he owns a lot of property." The sick sensation in his gut swam faster.

"Yes." She leaked the word out slowly, as though she could tell he was working something out in his mind.

"Earlier, you told me ketamine is used in designer drugs, and it's frequently stolen from veterinary clinics. You said John and Deacon had both gone to the same guy for advice and they should have stayed away."

"What are you thinking?" Lucas straightened and glanced around them as though he expected an assault at any second.

Maybe he should.

"A couple of years ago, I introduced John to a guy who lives in Raeford and has a lot of land. A guy who wouldn't have any problem getting whatever he wanted from a vet clinic." A guy who'd befriended Travis then tried to urge him to return to his own addictions, likely so he could drag him even lower, creating one more customer.

A guy who, when they saw him hours after John died, had hands bruised and cut more like a fistfight than a dogfight.

In a flash of clarity, Travis remembered where he'd seen their hooded stalker before. At Meredith's clinic. One of the vet techs. Until their last few encounters, the young man had always been smiling and friendly. His scowl in the shadows of the yard light at Casey's grandfather's house had been anything but.

Travis turned his face to the sky, wishing he had the words to pray but coming up empty. Let him be wrong. Let it be a stranger. But deep inside where he couldn't deny, he knew there was too much circumstantial evidence for it to be anyone else.

"Travis?" Casey laid a hand on his arm, drawing him into the moment. "You said you introduced John to him? I was listening to one of my interviews with John earlier, and he said the man he trusted had been introduced to him by a former team leader."

He exhaled loudly, and the guilt he'd been fighting washed back to knock him down like a rogue wave. He'd missed all the signs pointing him straight to the truth. Now one man was dead and another was battling for his life. "I don't think John said 'bet.' It was 'vet.' And I know exactly who he was warning us about."

In Kristin's small kitchen, the faded light of early evening leaked between the plantation blinds, muting the edges of the cabinets and casting the room in shadows. Nobody had bothered to turn on the lights, and the darkness grew heavier by the second, tempered by the streetlights popping on outside.

Travis slid away from Kristin's small kitchen table and stretched out his legs, his boot brushing Casey's.

Even brief contact was too much. She tucked her feet under her chair and leaned forward, bracing her elbows on the table. He'd touched her enough today. The warmth of his lips on hers lingered, and hopefully her cheeks weren't red enough to let the whole room know what she was thinking. With her insides all knotted, she never should have let him kiss her, but the longer they were around each other, the harder it was for her to keep her distance and the more she wanted to abandon her dreams to go chasing after his.

Except even he didn't know what his were anymore.

It didn't help the way the pain on his face made her want to comfort him. They'd all had to go to work after Travis's revelation about Meredith and Phil, and the afternoon had dragged on longer than any she'd ever known. He'd insisted on following her to Kristin's house. Reluctantly, she'd let him, but his silence since they'd arrived made her wonder more than once why he'd bothered. It had taken all her willpower not to reach out to him, but after the way he'd kissed her this morning and she'd responded, physical contact wasn't something either of them could handle.

They'd come to Kristin's house with Lucas and were all gathered in the kitchen, trying to land on a strategy. So far, they'd come up empty.

On the other side of the small round table, Kristin rolled an orange between her palms. She'd eaten two since the group had come together less than an hour ago.

"I don't know how you do it." Travis let a smile ghost his features.

Casey, Kristin and Lucas all swirled their heads toward him.

Lucas quirked an eyebrow from where he leaned

against the kitchen counter nearby. "How who does what?"

Dipping his head toward Kristin, Travis said, "I don't know how Kristin eats so many oranges. You got a cast-iron stomach?"

"Maybe." She rolled the fruit across the table to him and held up her hand for him to toss it back. She caught it neatly and ran a thumbnail along the peel. "Stress eating. I thought when we put my brother's killer away we were done with this kind of stuff. A girl can only take so many assassination attempts in her inner circle, you know?"

Kristin started to dig her thumb into the orange, but Lucas crossed the room in two strides and took it away. "Enough's enough. I'm cutting you off."

"Fine." She huffed then turned to Casey, her amusement evaporating as she returned to their earlier conversation. "I think you should tell the police."

"Wait. What?" Travis laughed, but the sound was bitter in the tense room. "This from the woman who absolutely refused to let any of us call the cops, even after someone broke into her house?"

Casey had never seen him so bitter, but it was there, the true testament to how much the situation was wearing on him. She wanted to lay a hand on his shoulder or take his hand in hers, to stand with him and to support him.

Then again, maybe it would do him some good to get this out of his system. Kristin was a strong woman. She could take it.

Apparently, Lucas agreed, because he didn't move from his position by the sink, simply crossed his arms and watched to see how the confrontation would play out.

"People change, Travis." Selecting another orange from the bowl on the table, she glanced over her shoulder at Lucas. "Don't worry, I'm not going to eat it." When she turned to Travis, her expression had grown serious. "I had my reasons for not calling. You? You have the look of a man about to go vigilante. Don't. Let the authorities take care of Phil and Meredith. You're too emotionally deep in this."

"What exactly am I supposed to tell them?" Travis shoved his chair away from the table and paced the length of the tile in the long, narrow room. "Everything we have is circumstantial. Other than a gut feeling and a few descriptions that sound like them but could also match two dozen other people, we've got nothing. The police won't do anything but maybe pay them a visit and ask a few questions, and those questions will send them straight underground. Or worse, make them more determined to silence whoever they see as a threat. I'm going to assume they think either John or Deacon fed information to Casey. That's why they stole her laptop, then when they couldn't get into it, came after her directly. If this is true and we want to stop them, then what we need is proof."

The way he paced like a caged tiger set Casey's nerves on edge. Kristin was right. He acted like a man at the end of his rope, likely to do anything to end what was happening to all of them. If he decided to take off after the Ingrams, Casey wasn't sure she could stop him.

She glanced at Lucas, who had straightened and was watching Travis as though he thought he might have to wrestle his friend into submission. The last thing she wanted to see was two buddies duke it out. "Can you call Marcus Brewer?"

Travis stopped and stared out the window above the kitchen sink, his profile tight. He dug his finger into his thigh and didn't say anything, just stared out the window.

"Travis?" She ached to go to him, and she might give in to the urge if he didn't come to his good senses soon.

"I don't know."

"Why not?"

"Because every time something happens, he's there. He's the only cop who was at all our crime scenes."

Glancing at Lucas, Casey chewed her next words carefully. They'd either calm Travis or set him off like a Fourth of July firework. "Sounds like you might be edging a little bit toward paranoid."

His head jerked up, his gaze hard on hers, but then he considered her before leaning against the kitchen counter to stare at the refrigerator. "Maybe." He glanced around at the small group. A full minute ticked by before he spoke again. "Know what? Maybe we all need a break. Things have been crazy the past few days and we're all seeing shadows where there aren't any." Shoving away from the counter, he walked to the door leading to the living room. "I'm out."

Lucas straightened, instantly alert. "To where?"

"Now you're paranoid. To my apartment, if it's okay with you. I need a shower and to get out of my uniform into civilian clothes. Follow me if you want, but it's your choice. I'll be back in an hour. Promise."

With a slow nod, Lucas watched him go.

Casey's muscles tensed, wanting to follow him to

make sure he was really as calm as he claimed to be. Since she'd nearly melted in his arms in the hospital lobby, he'd been distant, like they'd never shared a kiss. Maybe walking away had been the right thing to do, even if it did hurt. He hadn't made up his mind yet what he wanted.

But he was a man in pain. And he was the man she loved. Since the day he'd walked out her door never to return, she had never felt so helpless. "So what do we do?"

Kristin shrugged as Lucas sat in the seat Travis had vacated. "We could call the police, but Travis is right. If they give us any credibility at all, they'll go question Phil and Meredith. That's not doing anybody any good. All it does is tell them we're onto them. Somebody's going to have to find a way to get real evidence."

"Or get Deacon to talk." Casey sighed and stood, Travis's restlessness transferred to her, driving a need to pace the floor in his footsteps. "Maybe if I go to the hospital and try to—"

"Don't even think about it," Lucas said. "Travis would kill me if I let you step foot into the hospital while he suspects Phil of being behind all this. He works there, and he knows the ins and outs of every hallway. It's walking into enemy territory if I ever saw it. He could make you vanish before anyone even knew you were there."

Like yesterday. Casey wrapped her arms tight around her stomach. What would have happened if Travis hadn't appeared when he had? Likely, she'd have followed Phil, enticed by the lure of some peace and quiet. He was definitely smooth, the kind of guy who invited trust. Like so many serial killers she'd read about over the years, he was the last one you'd ever suspect. Now, safe in Kristin's kitchen, the pointed questions he'd asked stood out like blazing fires in the night. And his invitation for coffee? Accepting likely would have ended with Travis searching forever but never finding her.

The thought left her even antsier than before. She paced to the window that faced the front yard and watched Travis back out of Lucas's driveway, then hang a right.

A right.

If he were truly going to his apartment as he'd said, he'd have made a left. The only reason he'd have to turn right was if he'd decided to take matters into his own hands.

He was going rogue, on his way to force Phil's hand. Alone.

# SIXTEEN

The outside lights of Ingram's Veterinary Center glowed brightly in the darkness after sunset. The center, on a parcel of farmland near Raeford, consisted of a small white brick clinic near the road for office visits and, toward the rear of the property, a large white barn where Meredith practiced her real joy, rehabilitating horses. On the other side of a grove of trees and out of sight of the road, the two-story white house stood in a large clearing.

The parking lot sat empty and the clinic lights were dark, but the barn doors stood wide open, light pouring out of the structure.

Travis had called ahead to Meredith and said he wanted to take her up on the offer to visit Gus, who he knew usually nosed around the clinic or the barn all day. Meredith had been excited to agree.

He'd hated using his dog as the excuse.

Kneading the steering wheel, Travis glanced at his phone on the passenger seat, where it buzzed for what had to be the twentieth time since he'd left Kristin's. Casey and Lucas, maybe even Kristin, were probably calling to talk some sense into him. He probably needed it, but he didn't want it. What he wanted was to get some hard evidence to take to the police and to end this thing, to make sure Casey was safe so he could spend a few days focused on praying about what to do next instead of constantly scanning for trouble.

With uncertain threats hanging over both of their heads, the last thing he could do before this was over was go to selection. He was supposed to report in a few days and, right now, moving on was the last thing he wanted to do.

So this had to stop. Tonight.

Now that he was here, he had no idea what his plan was. The whole drive, he'd known he wanted to question Meredith apart from Phil, but exactly how to broach the subject had eluded him. He killed the engine on the truck and reached for the door handle, hesitating as he scanned the buildings.

He should have brought Lucas along. Backup was never a bad thing, but if this went south, he wanted to know the only one in danger was himself. And since, based on the time his phone had started ringing, he didn't have much of a head start, he'd better get moving.

As he pushed the truck door open, a figure appeared around the corner of the clinic, a shadow in the darkness until the person stepped into the circle of floodlights near the parking lot.

Meredith.

Dressed in what looked to be old jeans and a plaid button-down shirt, she looked every bit the farm girl cleaning out stables, not the murderous leader of a drug ring. Travis cast up a quick prayer the woman he'd known for years was innocent before he exited the truck.

She met him at the front bumper, swiping her hands down her jeans before she gave him a quick hug. "I knew you wouldn't be able to resist the memory of Gus's puppy-dog face for long. He's roaming around here somewhere. I tried calling him when you pulled in, but he's probably out in the woods chasing squirrels before they bed down for the night. Either that or he's at the house waiting for his supper. He's pretty good about knowing when it's quitting time, so I'm guessing he'll come charging in here any second. Come on out to the barn. I'm about to shut down for the night, and he'll definitely come running when he sees those lights go out. He's a smart pup."

For a moment, the prospect of seeing Gus drove away the more serious reasons he'd driven out to Meredith's. The dog had been his buddy for years, until he'd deployed for the third time and realized his coming and going was growing harder on the dog as he grew older. Travis had thought it was for the best, but now the idea he might have dumped his best friend off with violent drug dealers was more than he could take. The angry fire he'd managed to bank flared, but headlights turning into the small gravel parking lot cleared his thinking and refocused him on the situation at hand. He had to be ready for anything, and there was no telling who was coming in...or why.

Meredith's nose wrinkled. "I hope that's not a late emergency call. I'm ready to go home and grab a few minutes of peace around the fire pit. Bet Phil would love it if you came along. He's missed hanging out with you, but never tell him I said so."

Fat chance. There were a very limited number of things he wanted to say to Phil Ingram, and none of them qualified as friendly conversation.

Travis eyed the approaching vehicle until it became clear it was a Jeep Wrangler.

Casey.

Travis tensed. The last thing he needed was for Casey to get caught in the cross fire if something happened tonight. There was no way he'd be able to focus on his self-driven mission if he had to keep a watchful eye on her.

She climbed from the vehicle almost before she killed the engine, not quite meeting Travis's eye. "Sorry I'm running late." Sliding in beside him, she slipped an arm around his waist like this was something they did all the time and planted a kiss on his cheek, her whisper warm against his ear. "You shouldn't have come alone."

With a smile he hoped wasn't as fake as it felt, he put an arm around her waist and squeezed tighter than he normally would, a silent reprimand for following him. His mind spun for a way to get her back into her Jeep and out of harm's way, but no plan formed. Instead, he held her as close as he could, praying for her safety.

Meredith arched an eyebrow but didn't comment on their behavior. "Nice to see you again, Casey. Y'all ready to see if we can get Gus to come running?"

"Gus, huh?" Casey kept her voice low, for Travis's ears only, as she tried to pull away from him.

He held her tight to his side, matching his pace with hers as they followed Meredith. He wanted Casey as close as possible, and simply beside him wasn't enough. If they were ambushed at any point on this little outing, he wanted to know exactly where she was.

Because he couldn't bear it if the worst happened and his reckless flight tonight ended with Casey's blood on his hands.

The drive out to Meredith Ingram's clinic had been an amusement-park ride of raging emotions, with anger leading the charge. Coming out here alone, without telling anyone where he was headed, was foolish on Travis's part.

But then she had to admit she'd done the same thing to Lucas and Kristin, slipping out while they were occupied with debating dinner, then shutting off her phone. She didn't want them in the middle of this, which was likely the exact reason Travis had tried to make this trip solo. Her friends had been through enough at the hands of a killer who had done his best to destroy Kristin. They deserved to stay out of the line of fire this time.

But that didn't mean she was going to let Travis go this thing alone.

The way his fingers dug into her waist as they followed Meredith said more than the words he was likely biting down on. He was upset with her for following him, but they could discuss it later. She hoped. Because tonight they either got all the answers they needed or they went down for the count trying.

This had to end tonight. Casey didn't think she could handle any more looking over her shoulder. And she sure didn't want to play these will-they-or-won't-they games with Travis any longer. There were some serious discussions to be had in the near future, and those discussions had nothing to do with drug dealers and murderers.

At the huge door to the barn, Meredith stopped and swept her hand toward the massive building. In another time, it would have been peaceful, the pristine white structure glowing with light inside and out, the faint earthy scent of hay and horses wafting on the breeze. "We painted since the last time you were out here, Travis."

"Looks good. Who did the heavy lifting?"

Casey would love to have the kind of calm that came across in his voice. The farther they got from the road, the more her legs wanted to turn and run for her Jeep. If only she were the kind of girl who carried a concealed weapon at all times. But here she was, unarmed and possibly chatting with a killer, and she was fairly certain Travis was no more prepared than she was.

"We had a paint party. My vet techs, a few people from the community, some volunteers..." Meredith walked inside and headed for a huge bank of light switches near the door, seemingly at ease with their visit this evening. "As soon as we shut these off, Gus ought to come running."

If Meredith killed the lights and ushered them out, gone was their chance to do any sort of investigating. Their trip out here would prove futile. Casey scrambled for a reason to poke around in the barn, breaking away from Travis and stepping into the brightly lit interior before he could react. "You work on horses, too, Meredith?"

"Family pets pay the bills, but horses are my first love." Meredith looked proud, innocent, nothing like a conniving killer should look.

Long ago, Casey had learned to read people. It helped in interviews to know who was telling the truth or who was uncomfortable with her questions. Meredith stood with an open stance, her expression betraying no tension. Either the woman was clueless to her husband's possible activities or she was a very, very good liar.

Either way, this might be their one opportunity to find out the truth. "I love horses. Used to ride when I was a kid. Mind if I peek at them, or are they too sick for company?" It was all she had. She shot a look at Travis. Maybe if she kept Meredith busy long enough, he could do a little exploring for anything at all out of the ordinary.

Meredith's face lit as though Casey had offered up her life's savings. "Most of them are here for checkups or healing from surgery. They'd all love a little bit of attention from somebody besides me, I'm sure." She aimed a finger at a cabinet next to Casey. "There're sugar cubes on the top shelf if you want to make some real friends."

The woman appeared completely innocent. Or maybe she was psychopathic. Casey tugged open the cabinet door and took her time reaching for the sugar cubes, surveying the contents of the shelves. Rolls of bandages, containers of sugar cubes and a few miscellaneous grooming supplies littered the metal shelves. Nothing seemed out of the ordinary for a horse barn. Grabbing a fistful of treats, she shut the door and turned to Travis, who was a few feet away staring at an open shelving unit.

Casey turned to follow Meredith, who was halfway up the aisle of the brightly lit barn, when a man walked in the doors at the opposite end of the building. He was tall and wiry, his dark hair long enough to touch his ears, his tanned skin an indication he spent his fair share of time outdoors. "Hey, Doc. You about ready to close shop for the day? I've got—" He stopped when he saw Casey, his gaze bouncing from her to Meredith, then over their shoulders to something behind them, his expression a cross between anger and fear as he froze in the doorway.

Meredith stopped walking. "Dylan? Is everything okay?"

Dylan's mouth opened, then closed as though he considered some sort of confession. But then, without uttering a word, he turned and fled the building as though fear itself chased him.

"What are you—" Meredith's words choked off as Travis tore past them at full speed, flying after Dylan.

He called over his shoulder. "Casey. Call the police!"

Both women froze, trying to make sense of the scene in front of them, before Meredith jogged halfway down the length of the barn, staring at the door as though she couldn't comprehend what she'd seen.

Casey grabbed her cell phone and pressed the numbers but hesitated before she completed the call. What did Travis want her to say? She had no idea what it was about this Dylan guy that had set him off. Something big had happened, but she wasn't sure what.

Turning toward Casey, Meredith walked halfway up the barn aisle but stopped, her arms out to her sides as though she had no idea what had happened right in front of her. "What is going on here?" She seemed more confused than angry, but then she stopped and looked at something behind Casey. "Do you have any idea what just happened?"

There was a shuffle behind Casey. She turned to

see who Meredith was talking to, but a click drowned the barn in darkness.

"Have you lost your mind?" Meredith's voice cut the blackness.

Panic surged through Casey, rooting her feet to the floor. She had to get moving. Someone was behind her and she couldn't see where. Breathing hard, she dodged sideways, away from the sound of feet pounding toward her, her shoulder colliding with a stall door and setting off a snort and a whinny from the horse inside. She held her cell phone tighter. Either she could turn it on and use it as a flashlight to locate the unknown person, or she could stay in the dark and try to make herself invisible until Travis returned.

She eased toward the door through which they'd entered, hoping whoever was looking for her would assume she'd run away instead of moving toward them.

But a beam of intense light swept the building and caught her in its circle.

Before she could duck, the light plunged closer and swung in an arc.

Pain coursed through her neck and shoulder. The cell phone fell from her hand as Casey dropped to her knees and Meredith shouted something she couldn't understand. Her mind screamed *flight* while her aching body fought to curl into a ball to deflect any more blows. Hands grasped her wrists, twisting them from her head. She fought, but a blow to the side of her head shot stars across her vision and she went limp, the pain too overwhelming to fight.

The weight moved, but then a pressure and a jabbing pain stabbed her in her arm. She tried to scream, but her body was overwhelmed by pain. For what felt like hours, her captor pinned her wrists to the floor, but then he backed away. Rolling to the side, Casey fought to stand, bracing herself against the horse stall, desperate to run for the door. The room receded, and she felt as though her body was no longer hers but her brain had floated into the rafters. Her arms were heavy. Her legs moved through invisible sludge. Nothing would obey her command.

From what seemed a huge distance, a voice shouted then grew muted. A male voice close by joined the fray, lost in a roar that grew louder as her limbs grew weaker and heavier. Casey slumped to the floor, sliding down the stall door, her jaw slack and her body paralyzed and unmoving as a figure leaned over her. A muffled scream from nearby cut off suddenly, and the world closed into darkness.

# SEVENTEEN

Travis ran headlong into the blackness of the woods before he stumbled over a tree root and stopped, scanning the shadows around him, listening for sounds of the man Meredith had called Dylan. The same man who had attacked them at least twice before.

Only the breeze in the trees came to him, much like it had at John's house a few days before. Travis turned slowly, trying to capture the sound of footfalls or movement in the low brush, but nothing unusual drifted his way. Either this Dylan character was superhuman fast, or he'd found a low hiding position somewhere among the trees, knowing Travis would have to search the darkness to find him.

He dug his palm into the rough bark of a pine tree, frustration and fear clawing at him. If he had all night, he'd flush out the man, but he didn't have that kind of time. He had to get to Casey. Leaving her alone with Meredith when he had no idea how deeply the other woman was involved had been risky, but he'd hoped to catch Dylan on the run, the one solid link they had to the attacks. He prayed she'd done as he'd asked and gotten off a call to the police.

In the near distance, limbs and ground cover crackled at the fast approach of something smaller than a man but bigger than a forest animal. Travis whipped toward the sound in time to be nearly knocked off his feet by a panting mass of muscle and fur.

Gus.

Sinking to his knees, Travis allowed himself a brief reunion with the Australian shepherd, receiving a face full of whimper-punctuated licks. The dog broke something inside him, releasing the tension he'd been holding close around his entire being. For a second, he buried his face in neck fur, but he had to cut the reunion short. "I promise more pets later, boy. Right now's not the time."

The dog sat as though he understood, and Travis stood, listening for any sound to indicate Dylan was circling back. Other than Gus's joyful panting, there was silence.

Turning in the direction of the clinic, Travis jogged into the clearing at the edge of the woods with Gus at his heels, wary of running too fast and trashing his ankle in a hole or on a root. As he broke into open air, his feet stuttered to a stop. The outside lights around the clinic near the road shone as brightly as they had earlier, but the barn was dark inside and out. No longer content with a slow jog, Travis pushed himself with all he had to the barn, not stopping until he was at the huge doorway.

The darkness of the massive interior was muted around the edges by the light filtering in from outside. The silence was heavy, broken by Gus's breathing and the soft whinnies of the horses Meredith housed in a few of the stalls. No sounds that could be identified as human caught his attention.

But someone had to be there. He'd left Meredith and Casey behind only moments before.

With Dylan lurking somewhere behind him and the unknown darkness in front of him, Travis was a wide-open target as a silhouette in the doorway, so he edged to the side and stood in the shadows by the wall, trying to filter out the animal sounds to hear anything else.

Maybe Meredith had shut the barn for the night and the women had gone to the clinic. They could be there, waiting for him to return from what Meredith likely thought was a wild-goose chase.

Except Travis had shouted to Casey to contact the police and he'd shown recognition of Dylan, the man who was doing at least some of Phil and Meredith's dirty work. He'd tipped his hand and left Casey alone with one of their prime suspects.

There was no win here, though. He couldn't have chased Dylan and stayed by Casey's side at the same time. But if he'd stayed at her side, he'd have lost his shot at taking down the man who had repeatedly attacked them.

Not that he'd succeeded.

Cold fear pumped through his veins. He wanted to call out to Casey, but not knowing what he was battling, he didn't dare.

Edging deeper into the barn, Travis kept his footfalls light and his ears open as he crept close to the stalls, trying to watch both behind him and in front of him. His eyes gradually adjusted to the dim light, allowing shadows to take shape, including a heap on the floor in the center of the aisle by the other door.

He wrinkled his forehead as Gus whimpered, sensing his tension. Travis laid a hand on the dog's head. There hadn't been anything there when he'd walked in with Casey and Meredith or when he'd taken off after Dylan. His leg muscles trembled. No. It couldn't be a body. It couldn't be Casey.

Casting aside the need for stealth, Travis bolted for the crumpled mass, he kneeled and reached out.

Before he could verify what the object was, Gus barked and a sound from the doorway lifted Travis's head. A man stood there, silhouetted against the dim lights from the clinic down the hill.

Travis scrambled to his feet. Rather than wait to see if the man was friend or foe, Travis rushed him, hoping for the element of surprise in the near darkness, and launched himself at center mass, but the man met him halfway. Dipping low, Travis drove his shoulder into the man's stomach and let momentum throw his opponent over his back.

The other man crashed to the floor as Travis stumbled forward, but Travis recovered first, whipping around and aiming a fist at where he assumed the head would be.

The other man rolled, and the blow glanced to the side. The punch threw Travis off balance and sent him sideways as his assailant bucked, throwing Travis from him and scrambling to his feet before slamming into Travis like a defensive lineman and crashing him backward into a stall door.

The air burst from his lungs in a rush as his shoulder blades hit the wood, his head glancing off the door hard enough to force deeper darkness into his vision.

Gus barked and snarled, but he didn't charge. Behind him, a horse neighed and snuffed, scuffling in the stall.

Travis tried to shake off the blow as he fought to stay upright, but his attacker grabbed him by the shirt front and threw him to the ground. Tucking his shoulder, he rolled sideways from the anticipated next move, kicking his leg up and connecting somewhere on his opponent's body.

The man roared and stumbled, but before he could charge again, sirens wailed from somewhere in the distance, close, but probably still a couple of minutes away. Lucas had likely called them when Travis didn't respond.

The figure paused and cursed under his breath before hesitating above Travis like he was debating whether to finish the job. With another curse, he took two steps backward, then turned and ran for the front door of the barn, disappearing near the woods.

Gus followed as far as the door, barking and whining.

Jumping to his feet, Travis tried to rush after him, but the blow to his head had been too much. Dizziness waved over him, and he grabbed for the nearest stall, bending at the waist and gulping air, trying to regain his equilibrium and to stop the world from spinning.

He stumbled forward, foot catching something on the floor and stuttering to a halt. He dropped to his knees, the cool hardness of the concrete sending pain into his legs. Running his hands along the object, he immediately recognized his worst fear.

This was a person, lying prone in the middle of the barn. Jerking his cell phone from his pocket, he pressed a button and turned the screen's light toward the figure, praying without coherent words or thoughts that he was wrong, that the outcome would be anything other than a person, and it would be anything in the world other than Casey.

The light was bright in the dimness, but as his eyes adjusted, adrenaline threatened to overwhelm him.

The red shirt, the blond hair… He grabbed her by the shoulder and gently rolled her toward him, but she was dead weight, gravity tugging her body away from him. He rested her on her back, and her head lolled toward him, eyes closed, a bruise forming along the side of her face to her temple.

Casey was barely breathing, but she was alive.

He looked at the barn door as Gus trotted over and sat next to Casey, nudging her with his nose.

The sirens grew louder as several vehicles turned into the clinic parking lot, their red, white and blue lights casting crazy shadows even from this distance. He'd have to leave her to call for help, but leaving her meant making her vulnerable if someone still lurked in the shadows.

Not leaving her meant help might be precious moments too late.

Brushing the hair from her face, he tore himself away and made his way to the wall to flip on the lights, illuminating the building like a beacon in the night, then stood in the doorway and called for help.

A group of men in the parking lot looked his way, then went into motion.

Travis didn't wait to see what they did. He simply dropped beside Casey and prayed.

But before he could do more than assure himself she really was still alive, the first responders rushed into the building, where they huddled around her and eased him out of the way.

He stood to the side, numb, Gus leaning against his leg. Once again, exactly like when the medics had taken over after the improvised explosive device ripped into Neil Aiken, Travis could only stand by helplessly and watch others try to save someone he was responsible for hurting.

# EIGHTEEN

Casey squeezed her eyes tighter, but the movement only made the pounding in her head worse. She tried to focus on the voices talking quietly around her. Who in the world would be in her bedroom and why did everything hurt so much?

She squinted harder then slowly peeked. Dim gray light surrounded her, the image hazy and wavering. Her body felt heavy, and the walls around her didn't look like any room she ought to be asleep in.

Gasping, Casey tried to breathe and sit up at the same time. Pressure on her face trapped her. She tried to swipe at it, to figure out where she was, but gentle hands wrapped around her wrists and pulled them down before someone appeared in her line of sight.

Travis.

Sinking into the pillow, she focused on his blue eyes, letting herself find peace in them like she hadn't truly allowed herself to in a long time. He said something, but it didn't register in the fog of her brain, and she drifted out of consciousness.

When she woke again, the room was quiet and her mind was less muddy, though her head still throbbed.

Whatever had pressed into her face was gone, but her mouth was dry and her nose burned. She glanced around the room, trying to take inventory of where she was. The drab walls. The machines beside her. The smell of antiseptic and plastic.

The hospital. Fear jolted her, and through the fog in her brain, she fought to remember the last thing that had happened. All she could conjure was a woman screaming as a huge room went dark.

She slid her hand sideways, looking for a way to raise the bed so she could see better, but a whisper and a soft rustle to her right stopped her. Footsteps crossed the room and something like a door opening broke the silence, but she couldn't quite see from where she lay what was going on.

Once again, Travis appeared, a soft smile lifting and easing the fatigue that etched lines into his face. "You're back."

"From where?" Her voice rasped, dry and scratchy.

"Only you can answer that. Want me to raise the bed so you can have some water?"

In her whole life, nothing had ever sounded better. "Please."

With a hum, the head of the bed lifted, and she could see the room. In the far corner, Lucas was crashed on a small vinyl love seat, oblivious to the world. A blanket lay crumpled beside him, evidence Kristin had probably been there, too.

Travis let her drink from a straw, and the cool water drenched a path down her parched throat. "What happened?"

"You've been in and out for a couple of hours. The doc said you probably wouldn't remember what landed you here. And even though he said you'd be fine eventually, it seemed like it took you six years to come around."

"From what?"

Two taps sounded at the door, and a nurse peeked in. "I hear someone's awake." Questions and vitals followed, wrapping the minutes in a whirlwind of discussions Casey's brain was too tired to catalog.

Finally, blessedly, everyone was gone, including Kristin and Lucas, whom the nurse had kicked out early on. She didn't know where they were, but she was more than happy to shut her eyes and relax, Travis's hand wrapped around hers, as they waited for the on-call doctor to make an appearance and do a more thorough exam.

"Did I hear the nurse say 'ketamine'?" It had been the one word to filter through what had felt like mild chaos. Casey had clung to it with a kind of fear, praying she'd heard wrong but knowing she hadn't.

"You remember going to Meredith's clinic?"

Casey nodded slightly, but the pain in her head kept her from too much enthusiasm. "You chased a guy out of the barn. The place went dark…" She squeezed her eyebrows together, fighting for the memory that was so tantalizingly close, then shook her head. "Then I was here, but it was like dreaming. Not being here but being here." Even now, wide awake, a slight panic shuddered through her at her own body's betrayal. "I'm guessing that was the drug?"

"Probably." He pulled his hand from hers and scrubbed it against a day-old beard. He still wore his uniform, the front covered in smudged dirt, hay clinging to some spots, as though he'd tumbled to the barn floor and spent a good deal of time there. His eyes were tired, his face haggard.

"You okay?"

He chuckled, his gaze finding hers and softening in a way she hadn't seen in a long time. "Now that you're awake."

Casey looked away, then gave up the fight and faced him again. He might be leaving, but he was here now. She'd live in what she had and deal with normal life later.

Except life without him would never be normal again.

She couldn't tell him, even though the ache in her chest matched the one in her head. "Did they catch Phil and Meredith?"

"They caught Dylan. According to him, Phil conveniently left this afternoon for a kayaking trip in the mountains. We doubt that's true, but we're looking to verify. Until he gets a lawyer, he's not saying much else."

So Phil was still out there, still possibly involved in everything that had happened. The thought of him skulking around somewhere ran electric fear through her, but the guarded expression on Travis's face stopped her. "Something else is bothering you."

He was silent for a long time, staring at the railing on the bed, his expression troubled, as though there was something he didn't want to say.

Casey wanted to hold her hand out to him, but her arm ached, and the IV impeded movement. If she was truly going to come out of this unscathed, then it wasn't her condition that darkened his features. Something else had to be bothering him, something he was hesitant to tell her.

Deacon.

Her heart squeezed. "Did someone make another run at Deacon?"

"What?" Travis seemed to return from far away. "Not that I know of."

"Then what?"

Leaning forward, he picked up her hand and laid his underneath, careful of the IV pumping liquid of some sort into her vein. He stared at their hands. "It's Meredith."

"She was the one who did all of this?" It couldn't be. She'd seemed so nice. When Travis had bolted after the man in the barn, her surprise had certainly appeared to be genuine. And the scream in the darkness had to have been hers.

"I don't know." His thumb stroked the side of her hand, sending a pulse of pleasure along her arm.

She had to ignore those feelings now, though. "Then what?"

"She's dead."

Casey froze, the words falling like ice into her being. More death. It was never going to stop. "What happened?" The question in a whisper around the pain in her throat, which had magnified into a baseball.

"While the paramedics worked on you, I talked to the police and told them what we suspected, how the man I'd chased out of the barn had mugged us, and had been at Deacon's and at your great-grandfather's house the night before. They—"

"What?" The words were a slap to the face. He'd

faced down danger—alone—at her family home and hadn't told her. "The man at the barn was at the house?"

Travis winced. "That's a story for later."

It sure was. And he'd better believe he was going to be telling it in full. She debated forcing it out of him now, but the pain hit her all over again. Meredith Ingram was dead. Everything else was trivial. "Then what?"

"They got a warrant and searched the barn and the clinic. I got a call from Marcus while you were out." He puffed out a deep breath and hesitated, the lines around his mouth growing deeper. "They found her in her office at the desk. He couldn't tell me too much, but it looks like suicide. She left a note on her computer confessing to everything including..." He trailed off and squeezed her hand, then shrugged like he was going to stop.

"You don't get to back off on me now, Heath."

He gave her a grim look, face tense and expression unreadable. "Your murder."

Casey's stomach clenched. She was going to be sick. She tried to sit higher, gasping for air, fighting nausea.

Lowering the bed rail, Travis eased around the lines running into her arm and sat beside her, wrapping his arms around her and holding her near, murmuring something she couldn't understand but that wound into her panic and wrapped around her heart, warming her from the inside out.

Ignoring the pain in her head, she turned her face into his shoulder and let him hold her, let him keep her safe. He was here for now, when she needed him. Tomorrow she'd figure out how to go forward without him when this was all over, even though the pain would be greater than anything in her body right now. "You found me."

He nodded once, then planted a kiss on the top of her head before resting his chin there, showing no signs of backing away. "Pretty sure nothing's ever scared me so bad in my whole life." His arms tightened around her. "It made me realize for certain that I never should have let you go in the first place."

The extra thump in her chest had nothing to do with the physical ordeal she'd been through. He'd admitted what she'd been needing to hear, had acknowledged with words that his feelings ran as deeply as hers. Burying her face in the space between his neck and shoulder, she closed her eyes and lost herself in the scent of his soap and the warmth of his arms. She took a deep breath that was all him. "I never should have let you walk away."

His arms tightened around her, but before he could say anything, a tap at the door broke the growing electricity between them.

Casey wanted to reel in the last thirty seconds and hold on to them. Somewhere deep inside, she knew they'd either just gained something she'd thought lost, or she'd lost something she might never get back.

A woman pushed the door open and stepped in, and Travis was instantly on his feet. "Dr. Walters."

She smiled at him then turned to look at Casey as a nurse came into the room behind her. "Good to see you're still awake."

Dr. Walters wasn't dressed like any doctor Casey had seen before. In jeans and a long-sleeved T-shirt, she looked as though she'd be more at home in a local restaurant than in the hospital.

"Excuse me for not being in full-on doctor mode." She smiled kindly and lifted an ID card she'd clipped to her shirt. "I promise I'm official. I'd been home long enough to change when I got the call you'd come all the way around and thought I'd drop by since we live around the corner."

Travis planted a kiss on the top of Casey's head and released her hand, backing away.

Casey wanted to lunge for him and hold on, to ask him what he'd been about to say, but her body likely wouldn't obey, which saved her the embarrassment of throwing herself at him.

He winked as though he could read her mind.

Glancing between them as though she knew she'd interrupted something, Dr. Walters finally turned to Travis. "Would you mind stepping out while we check on her? If you want, you can bring her some real food from the café downstairs, since the only thing she's likely to get from the nurses this time of night is a turkey sandwich that's been sitting in a fridge for a while. Something light, though. Soup or a chicken breast."

Food. The thought of it set a longing inside her, and it screamed for satisfaction. She'd let Travis step out for a few minutes, if he promised to bring her food. They could talk later. Physical needs took precedence. "Yes, please."

Travis grinned. "I'll be back in fifteen minutes. Lucas and Kristin should be here soon, too. They ran to grab me real clothes and to check on Gus." He gave her a look loaded with a sadness Casey couldn't quite read, then slipped out the door, leaving her to face the doctor and to wonder exactly what he had on his mind.

# NINETEEN

In the hallway, Travis leaned against the wall beside Casey's door and let the building hold him up, tilting his head toward the ceiling exactly as he had outside Deacon's room the night before. It felt like years had passed. Last night, he'd never dreamed the next time he saw this place it would be at Casey's side.

He let the wall hold his weight, digging his boot heels into the tile floor. Bad enough he'd confessed his mistake in leaving her. Worse hearing her agree. He'd been about to spill everything to Casey, to tell her he still loved her and wanted to talk about what came next when the doctor had interrupted them.

It was probably a good thing. Lucas's assertions that fear was running Travis's life in God's place had plagued him. Seeing Casey slumped on the concrete floor of the barn had assaulted him with doubt. He loved her, but he'd almost lost her. He wanted to be with her, but he didn't even know what his own future looked like.

Watching the EMTs and the paramedics take over Casey's care had driven his fear home, but now he understood what Lucas had been trying to tell him. He could leave her now and hurt them both, or he could be with her for as long as God gave them, living in the kind of joy only Casey brought him. From the recesses of his memory came a verse he'd once heard, something about perfect love casting out fear.

He hadn't loved Casey before, not in a selfless way. He'd loved how she made him feel, but he'd never spent much time considering her. Now, having nearly lost her and putting himself in the line of fire for her, he knew this was what love really was. Sacrificing. Fearless.

He loved Casey Jordan...but he still didn't know if God intended for them to be together, and he refused to do anything that didn't have God's approval.

Travis pushed away from the wall and trudged for the bank of elevators. He punched the button for the main floor and stared at the door. *Lord, what do You want from me? I know what I want, but I'm more confused than ever about whether or not I deserve it. Forgive me for listening to myself instead of You. I'm tired of talking. Help me listen.*

Silence. What had he expected? A voice to fall out of heaven? A map to appear on the wall? If only God would speak as epically as He used to, in audible voices or writing on stone.

When the doors slid open on the ground floor, Travis headed for the cafeteria, wishing the coffee bar was still open for some decent caffeine to keep him awake as the clock crept into the later hours of the night. He needed his wits about himself if he was going to fight his own desires yet still sit vigil with Casey.

"Travis."

His name in a familiar voice from across the room stopped him, sheening his muscles with the readiness to fight. The last time someone had hailed him in this lobby, it had been Phil. Travis balled his fists, prepared for confrontation, and whipped toward the sound.

Marcus Brewer strode across the lobby, dressed in jeans and a plaid button-down shirt, an odd sight out of uniform.

Travis relaxed. "Man, you shouldn't yell at a guy as jumpy as I am."

"Lay off the caffeine then." Marcus held out his hand, gripped Travis's quickly, then pulled him in for a one-armed hug before he let go. "How are you holding up? I heard about your girlfriend. Thought I'd swing by and offer you a little moral support, see if you needed me to hang out awhile and keep watch while you took a break."

Travis nodded slowly, the action thawing some of the tension inside him. There was something about friends made in the army, the brotherhood that lasted even after the combat gear was stowed and the assignments brought separation. He'd been wrong to suspect Marcus earlier, driven by frustration and fear. The other man's selflessness was almost more than Travis could bear after the roller coaster he'd ridden for the past three days. "Appreciate it." Two words were the best he could do when he was exhausted and his emotions rode too close to the surface.

"No worries, man." Marcus clearly understood what Travis wasn't saying. He shifted his weight onto his heels.

"Any word on Phil?" Travis didn't know if the police bought the story that Phil was out of town, but he sure didn't. He'd fought Dylan the night before. The man he'd wrestled with in the barn was definitely someone else, someone built exactly like Phil Ingram.

Scratching behind his neck, Marcus tilted his head. "Can't comment. Can say the last I heard was his phone pinged near Johnson City."

Travis exhaled the breath it felt like he'd been holding for hours, letting his shoulders sag. With Johnson City a four-hour drive away, Phil couldn't possibly be close enough to harm Casey tonight.

But if he really was on the other side of the state, who'd attacked Casey and killed Meredith? While it did appear Dylan was responsible for some of the dirty work, the kind of violence inflicted on John was a whole lot more personal than a hired hand would have dealt out. And he'd never believe that Meredith was behind all of this. The confession on her computer— to a murder that had not yet been committed—made him even more certain of his old friend's innocence.

Marcus snapped his fingers in front of Travis's face. "You taking a space walk, Heath?"

"No. I thought the puzzle was all together but I'm still missing some pieces."

"Let the professionals handle it. You take care of getting your girlfriend well."

"She's not…" Travis shook his head, ignoring the way his heart called him a liar. "Never mind. It's complicated."

Marcus's laughter echoed off the window to their left, which looked out into a small atrium. The few people in the lobby turned to toss them a wave. "Man, you ain't even right. You're in love with the woman. Knew it from the minute I saw you staring at her at Winslow's house. You'd have taken out anybody who dared to even look at her sideways. So why aren't you telling her? Get over yourself, haul your rear into town first thing in the morning and buy her a ring. Done and done."

"Says the man who quit the army because his wife couldn't hack it." Travis winced at the bitterness in his own words. A low blow, coming at the guy's wife, especially when Travis had never even met her. "Dude, I'm sorry. That was wrong."

"With all you've been through, you're due a few sharp words." Shrugging, Marcus lifted a slight smile. "Got a minute?"

"If you don't mind walking with me to grab Casey something to eat."

"I've got nothing but time."

They kept pace with one another in the hallway, their footfalls unusually loud in the silence.

Marcus paused, taking something from the quiet before he spoke. "Look, I like to tell people my wife's the reason we settled down, but truth is, I didn't want to play the game anymore. I still wanted to serve, but I wanted to be around when the kids started school and not have to worry about shuffling them from place to place. Besides, some guys go in knowing they want the military for a career, and some only want a few years to get direction." He held up a hand as though he thought Travis was going to interject. "Not a thing wrong with either way of life. God's got a different calling for each of us, you know?"

Travis nodded, trying to figure out where this was going. "But what if you're not sure anymore what you're being called to?"

"You mean you can't decide whether to stay in or get out?"

"I'm staying, no doubt. More like what I'll do if I stay."

"Thought you wanted to be an infantry first sergeant. Ride the ride for twenty or more then retire. Isn't that what you told me pretty much every day we were stationed together?"

It's what he'd always thought. Until a hot desert day when everything he thought he knew blew away with a roar.

"Let me ask you something." Marcus stopped in the middle of the brightly lit hallway and turned toward Travis. "Deep in the deepest part of you, what is it you really want? I'm not talking about what somebody told you or what you think you're obligated to do or what some TV show said was right. What's the dream God put in you, Heath? The one you know is all yours. The one that, when you think about it, it brings you peace. Because let me tell you something… If you can't find peace, then you probably aren't on the path God created you for." He shrugged and grinned, poking his index finger into Travis's biceps. "Then again, brother, those are my two cents. Take 'em or leave 'em."

Travis was too stunned to speak. How was it he'd finally promised God he'd listen, and He'd answered so quickly?

And how was it God sounded an awful lot like Marcus Brewer?

Travis stood in the middle of the hallway, looking first toward the cafeteria and then back the way he'd come, toward Casey and staying in the infantry and the peace he'd been chasing for years.

In front of him, Marcus chuckled then rolled his eyes. He grabbed Travis and turned him toward the lobby, then pointed over his shoulder. "That way, brother. I'll find you and bring some food with me. You go do what I think you've known all along you need to do. You worry about your woman, and you let me and mine worry about Ingram."

Travis's muscles practically itched to run to Casey, but something held him in place. A thought he couldn't quite grab onto.

Marcus shoved him. "Get your feet moving. She's waiting."

"No. There's something…" Travis tried to shove his emotions aside to clear his thoughts. "Meredith. It's something Meredith said when we were at the barn."

"What?" Marcus's mirth disappeared, and his hand went for his hip pocket. He pulled out his cell phone, thumb poised to dial. "I know that look. You're about to give us what we need to tie this thing up."

Closing his eyes, Travis pictured the walk from the parking lot to the barn and Meredith turning toward him. *I'm ready to go home and grab a few minutes of peace around the fire pit. Bet Phil would love it if you came along.*

There it was. Phil had been at the house when Travis and Casey were there, but he hadn't made an appearance. Even now, with his wife dead from what looked to be a suicide, he was conspicuously absent. He'd had time to murder Meredith and vanish before the police gained a warrant to access the clinic where she was found. And sizing up the man he'd done battle with in the barn, he was almost certain… He'd been fighting Phil for Casey's life.

Travis paced backward along the hallway, each step faster than the last. "Phil's in town. Casey needs protection. Deacon, too. Trust me." Without waiting to see how Marcus reacted, Travis turned and ran for the stairs. Phil worked in the hospital and knew how to get around without being seen. He had wide-open access to Deacon and now, to Casey.

Travis's steps echoed in the hallway as his lungs protested the exertion. He had to get to Casey before Phil finished what he'd started.

Casey stared at the blank TV screen and wished Travis would hurry. Dr. Walters hadn't been in the room two minutes before her pager went off and she'd excused herself, leaving Casey alone. Lying here with no backup and tethered to the bed by an IV line only hours after someone had tried to kill her made her edgy, and the lingering effects of the ketamine weren't helping. If she knew where her cell phone was, she'd call Travis and be every bit the pitiful specimen of human being she felt like at the moment, telling him to forget the food and come hold her hand because she was afraid of the dark.

Stupid. Casey slid higher in the bed and pressed the button to ease herself upright. She was a soldier. Maybe not a battle-hardened Ranger like Travis and Lucas, but she was still a soldier, and this was definitely behavior she ought not to fall prey to.

One thing she did know for certain, though… As soon as Travis returned and they were alone, she was going to tell him the truth she'd started to tell him when Dr. Walters stepped in. It might be cliché, but fighting for her life had caused something inside her to click into place. Her value wasn't in the eyes of others, and she'd spent far too long thinking it was. When she'd dated Travis, she'd been in awe, always wondering what a man like him could possibly see in her, always believing he'd walk away one day because he'd suddenly awakened and realized he could do better. She'd never seen it before, but lying here now after almost losing everything, she knew her value, and it wasn't in the eyes of men. It was in the eyes of God.

Her love for Travis had been selfish, seeking validation and completion that he was never created to give her. Now, she knew... She loved him for the man he was, the one who made her laugh, the one who always had her back, the one she'd sacrifice for if she had to.

If Travis rejected her, it would cut to her soul, but she'd survive. She didn't need him to make her whole, but she wanted him in her life because, without him, life would be a whole lot emptier. And it would be missing a huge, crucial piece.

As if on cue, two taps sounded, but no one came in. Maybe he thought Dr. Walters was still in the room. "It's fine. They're gone."

The door edged open and a man slipped in, shutting the door behind him before recognition kicked in.

It wasn't Travis.

Phil Ingram stood at the foot of the bed, eyeing her with a grim tilt to the side of his mouth.

Casey tried to scream, but he was next to her in an instant, his hand over her mouth, pressing her against the bed. She struggled, her limbs weak from the effects of the drugs still lingering in her system and no match for the man who had several inches and several pounds on her.

The monitors beside her had to be registering her change in breathing and heart rate, pinging to the nurses that something was wrong. One of them had to check on her soon. Casey just had to stay alive until they did.

With the last fight she had in her, Casey twisted her head and clamped down on Phil's hand hard, trying to hold on. If he was going to kill her, she'd be sure he left plenty of DNA evidence behind.

With a silent growl, he tore his hand from her mouth, then backhanded her. The force to the side of her face knocked her sideways, pain dragging tears from her eyes and leaving her dazed, stealing what remained of her fight.

While she struggled to recover, he punched buttons on the monitors and turned to face her, breathing heavily, the hatred he exuded thickening the air in the small room until Casey felt as though she couldn't survive under the suffocating weight of it. "This would have been a whole lot easier if you hadn't fought." He swiped at the sweat on his forehead with his injured hand, leaving a streak of blood behind.

Casey fought the pain and panic that paralyzed her, trying to get her mouth to work, her arms to move, but like in every nightmare she'd ever had, her body refused to respond, and her mouth refused to make a sound.

Keeping a hard eye on her, Phil reached into his pocket and produced a large syringe filled with a cloudy liquid. "I just left Deacon Lewis's room. Chances are, he's gone or close to it. Once we're done here and once Travis goes home and overdoses in his grief, everyone will think all this death rests squarely on Meredith's shoulders." He pulled the cap from the vial, then, like a snake, reached over and grabbed Casey's arm, jerking it toward him, the IV in her hand twisting and bringing more breath-stealing pain. She struggled, but he squeezed her wrist until it throbbed.

He laid the needle against the vein on the inside of her arm.

The door opened. "Casey, you—"

Phil jerked, and the needle pierced Casey's skin then fell away, clattering to the floor.

Travis.

He filled the doorway, his face hard with rage. "Back away, Ingram, or I'll kill you myself." Keeping his eye on Phil, he tilted his head and yelled into the hallway, "Call security!"

Phil took the opportunity to lunge for the door, but Travis was ready for him. He stepped to the side. As soon as Phil was close, Travis grabbed him and, using the other man's momentum, swung him into the frame of the door with a loud crash, then let him slump to the floor in the hall before both men dropped from view.

Casey sank into the bed and let her eyes slip closed, tears sliding down her cheeks as shouts and footsteps blasted in from the hallway. Ebbing adrenaline left her limp and shaking, unable to take in the chaos around her.

"Casey." A familiar voice broke through the noise, guiding her into reality. She opened her eyes to find Travis standing over her. "You're safe. Phil's in custody. It's over."

She smiled what felt like the first smile she'd been able to muster in days. Not quite able to believe the threat was really over, she reached for him with a trembling hand. "Never, ever leave me alone again."

He rested his forehead against hers as more bodies poured into the room. His whisper was for her alone. "I won't. I promise."

# TWENTY

Casey shut the door behind her mother and dropped her head against the metal for a moment, reveling in the silence before she headed to the kitchen to find something to drink. Sometimes her throat ached so much she felt as though she'd never get enough water ever again.

In the living room, Travis dropped onto the couch and snapped his fingers, calling Gus over. The dog had been a constant companion ever since Casey had left the hospital, apparently slipping back into Travis's life as though he'd never left.

It made Casey a little bit jealous, the way Gus got to be so close to him while she had to stay at arm's length. He'd kept his distance since Phil had been arrested, but that might be because they hadn't been alone since. Her mother had arrived and hovered as though Casey were an infant all over again. Although she appreciated the love from Mom, what she really wanted was Travis all to herself.

And now that her mother had decided to make a run to the grocery store, Casey had what she wanted and had no idea what to do with it.

Gus whined softly as Travis rubbed his ear, as

though he couldn't get enough. Travis looked the same way. He'd found his best friend again, and it showed. He looked up from his seat in the den and caught her watching. "Was Kristin as fun when she got out of the hospital as you are?"

From the kitchen, Casey looked over the counter and widened her eyes in mock fear. "She was terrible. So, so terrible. It's a wonder Lucas could bear to be around her." She turned to hide her grin and tugged open the refrigerator door, her body still protesting the abuse from several days ago, her arm screaming a bruised reminder of the rough treatment it had endured at Phil Ingram's hand.

That first night in the hospital, she hadn't been able to sleep, still convinced somehow the man would evade the police and find her. Even with her friends in the room, she'd felt exposed and vulnerable. Last night, with Kristin in the spare room and Travis on her couch, had been a little bit easier. Still, she jumped at every sound and constantly had to remind herself nobody was hunting for her anymore.

Phil was in custody and, once Dylan had realized the other man was caught, he'd started talking, probably hoping for a plea deal for his cooperation. Marcus had dropped by last night to fill them in on the details.

Phil had read Casey's story on recovering addicts and realized both Deacon and John had talked to her. Believing her latest conversations with them would out him for stealing medications from his wife to sell on the street, he'd first had Dylan steal her laptop to find out what she knew. When it was password protected, he'd gone after John, beating the man to death in a rage when he let slip he may have mentioned Phil to Casey in a prior interview and he'd also put her in touch with Deacon.

Phil had intended to do away with Deacon before he could talk, but he'd miscalculated what it would take to kill the bigger man.

He'd gone straight after Casey, believing she knew enough to take him down. He'd drugged her in the barn with the intention of hauling her away and killing her where the deed would leave no evidence connecting her to him, but Travis had found her while Phil was dealing with Meredith, who'd figured out what he was doing.

And now, it was over.

Except the fear still lingered. And so did Travis's impending departure.

"There's no shame in counseling, you know." Travis's voice was too close behind her.

Casey jumped and slammed the refrigerator door shut, then leaned her forehead against the cool stainless steel, absentmindedly running her fingers across Gus's head when he nudged her knee. "Who said I needed help? I'm fine." Right now marked the first time she'd been alone with Travis in days, and here she was pacing and thinking instead of looking him in the eye to tell him everything she'd realized in the hospital. He left for selection in two days, and if she didn't say it now, she might never get the chance.

Instead, they were discussing her mental state. This was all going sideways.

Laying a gentle hand on her shoulder, Travis turned Casey toward him and wrapped his arms around her, pulling her close. "You jump when the a/c kicks on. You pace your room all night. And you stood there for about three minutes staring into the fridge without moving." He slid back but kept his hands locked at her waist, then planted a kiss on her forehead. "Talk to somebody."

"I'm talking to you right now."

"You know what I mean." He released her to lean against the opposite counter, crossing his arms, making his biceps stand out more than they usually did. "There's no shame in asking for help. If I'd been smart and not so determined to be a gung ho GI Joe, I might have talked to someone sooner and not almost derailed my life the way I did."

Easing herself onto the counter next to the fridge, Casey slid back and tapped her heels against the bottom cabinet door, trying to appear unaffected by the change in his tone. Hope surged. Maybe this was the conversation she'd been longing to have. "How did you almost derail your life?"

Travis crossed the small kitchen in two steps and leaned against the counter between her knees, planting his hands on either side of her hips. The blue in his eyes deepened in a way she'd seen before and once thought she'd never see again. The shiver that ran along her spine this time wasn't fear. It was much more pleasant.

He planted a kiss on her nose, then tipped his head until their foreheads met, his lips a breath away from hers. "I walked out on you because I was afraid and thinking I needed to be a different man if I wanted to be who God intended."

Casey's heart stuttered against her ribs. If she tilted her head even half an inch, his lips would be on hers. But she needed to hear what he had to say, even if being this close to him was exquisite torture. She swallowed against the pain in her throat and wrapped her arms around his neck. "That was wrong?"

"Very wrong." His arms slid around her, and he tugged her closer. "Because the man I'm supposed to be is the one standing here right now, with you."

She might pass out if her breathing got any more shallow. "What about—"

"Wait." Stepping back, he opened his hand. A sapphire ring wreathed with small diamonds rested on his palm.

Casey's breath hitched, tears pushing behind her eyes. "That's my grandmother's engagement ring. How—"

"Your mom brought it with her." He held the ring out to her. "Case, I've been an idiot, totally clueless about what God wanted for my life until now. Because now I know it's you. I love you, and I'm not leaving. I'm staying here as long as the army will let me, and I'm really, really praying that when they tell me it's time to go, you'll be packing your rucksack right beside me."

A week ago, she'd have said she'd given up on her heart's secret dream, yet here it was in front of her, asking for her heart. "Yes."

Travis grinned and slipped the ring onto her finger, then planted a kiss on her wrist.

Everything else Casey had to say could wait, because Travis was saying it all for her. With a peace deep in her soul, Casey pressed her lips to his and met him all the way, finally, completely, finding the home she'd always dreamed of.

\* \* \* \* \*

*If you enjoyed CALCULATED VENDETTA,*
*look for these other military suspense books*
*from Jodie Bailey:*

*FREEFALL*
*CROSSFIRE*
*SMOKESCREEN*
*COMPROMISED IDENTITY*
*BREACH OF TRUST*
*DEAD RUN*
*Available now from Love Inspired!*

*Find more great reads at www.LoveInspired.com*

Dear Reader,

When I was little, we were vacationing at the beach. My mom found a piece of sea glass. Sand and surf had smoothed the bumps and edges of a broken Coke bottle.

She handed it to me and said, "We're like this glass. We start out broken from sin. Jesus is like the waves and the sand, making us shiny and beautiful."

It was a lesson I've always remembered. The greatest thing Mom taught me was God is in everything, and He is everywhere. If we wait for Him, He will reveal Himself.

I like to think she learned that from my grandmother, who once called and said, "I was making the bed, and the way the light came through the window and hit the bedspread... I sat down and cried, because I felt how much God loves me."

Funny thing is, I've stood in our kitchen—which used to be hers—as the light fell over the butcher-block island and felt that same thing.

God loves you right where you are. He is a Zephaniah 3:17 God: "The Lord your God in your midst, the Mighty One, will save; He will rejoice over you with gladness, He will quiet *you* with His love, He will rejoice over you with singing."

I hope you will take a few minutes alone with Him and let Him tell you how much He loves you!

I also hope you will drop by and say hello over at

www.jodiebailey.com or at jodie@jodiebailey.com.
I'd love to hear how you've seen God in the small
things, too!

*Jodie*

# COMING NEXT MONTH FROM
## Love Inspired® Suspense

### Available June 6, 2017

## SPECIAL AGENT
*Classified K-9 Unit* • by Valerie Hansen

When K-9 unit Special Agent in Charge Max West heads to California with his dog to track down a bomber, he finds himself protecting horse trainer Katerina Garwood—a woman who might be his number one suspect.

## ROCKY MOUNTAIN SABOTAGE
### by Jill Elizabeth Nelson

After the private plane that Lauren Carter, her mother and executives from her stepfather's company are taking is sabotaged, they're forced to land in an abandoned mining town. And if they want to survive, Lauren and former air force pilot Kent Garland must catch the killer in their midst.

## LANCASTER COUNTY RECKONING
### by Kit Wilkinson

Darcy Simmons's father—who became Amish when he entered Witness Protection—is in a coma, and the criminals who attacked him are after *her* to produce the evidence he was hiding. Now the only person she can depend on to keep her safe is Amish farmer Thomas Nolt.

## HIDDEN LEGACY
### by Lynn Huggins Blackburn

When Caroline Harrison and her adopted son are targeted by someone after the baby, she'll do anything to protect him—even if it means turning to her high school crush, detective Jason Drake, for help.

## HIGH DESERT HIDEAWAY
### by Jenna Night

Caught accidentally overhearing a crime being planned, Lily Doyle flees for her life—and is saved by deputy sheriff Nate Bedford. With Lily's life on the line, Nate insists on hiding her until the criminals are found. But that may be harder than he thinks.

## DEADLY MEMORIES
### by Mary Alford

With no memories of her past and a child to protect, Ella Weiss doesn't know what to do: trust CIA agent Kyle Jennings's offer of help, or her captor's claim that the only way to save the child is to kill Kyle.

---

**LOOK FOR THESE AND OTHER LOVE INSPIRED BOOKS WHEREVER BOOKS ARE SOLD, INCLUDING MOST BOOKSTORES, SUPERMARKETS, DISCOUNT STORES AND DRUGSTORES.**

LISCNM0517

# Get 2 Free Books,
## Plus 2 Free Gifts—
### just for trying the Reader Service!

Katerina Garwood was halfway between one of the stables and the house, heading for her old suite, when she saw an imposing black vehicle pass beneath the ornate wrought iron arch at the foot of the drive. Unexpected company was all she needed. If her father came outside to see who it was and caught her trespassing on his precious property he'd be furious. Well, so be it. There was no way she could run and hide in time to avoid encountering the new arrival—and perhaps her irate dad, as well.

Chin high, she paused in the wide, hard-packed drive and shaded her eyes. The SUV reminded her of one that had assisted the county sheriff on the worst day of her life. The day when all her dreams of a happy future had vanished like a puff of smoke.

Dark-tinted windows kept her from getting a good look at the driver until he stopped, opened his door and stepped partway out. Prepared to tell him to go to the house if he needed to speak to someone in charge, she took one look and was momentarily speechless. The blond, blue-eyed man was so imposing and had such a powerful presence he sent her usually normal reactions whirling. When he spoke, his deep voice magnified those unsettling feelings.

"Katerina Garwood?"

"Do I know you?"

"No, but I know you. I'm Special Agent West. I'd like to talk to you about Vern Kowalski."

"I have nothing to say." She started to turn away.

"This is not a social call, Ms. Garwood." He flashed a badge and blocked her path. "I suggest you reconsider."

"FBI? You have to be kidding. I am so normal, so boring, that until recently people hardly noticed me."

"They do now, I take it."

She blushed and rolled her eyes. "Oh, yeah."

"Then you'll understand why I need to speak with you."

*Don't miss*
*SPECIAL AGENT by Valerie Hansen,*
*available wherever*
*Love Inspired® Suspense ebooks are sold.*

www.LoveInspired.com